AFTERMATH &
UNDERCOVER

ALSO BY VANESSA KIER

AFTERMATH & UNDERCOVER

VANESSA KIER

CONTENTS

AFTERMATH

THE SURGICAL STRIKE UNIT BOOK FIVE

CHAPTER ONE

Siobahn Murphy did not like unsolved mysteries. She never put a book down in the middle of a cliff-hanger. No matter how desperately she needed the facilities, she wouldn't leave a movie theater if a major plot point was about to be revealed. Friends had learned not to play board games with her unless they wanted a cutthroat fight. Worse, she was damn competitive when it came to figuring out whodunnit.

All of that made her an excellent investigative journalist, if she did say so herself. Her ex-husband, wherever his philandering soul might be, had called her a damned bulldog who didn't have the sense to take herself out of the line of fire. Given that he'd died in Iraq trying to pull one of his men out of range of a sniper's bullet, he hadn't really been one to talk.

Nothing sent her journalist's instincts into overdrive faster than receiving negative attention from the government or law enforcement. A few minutes ago, a team of FBI agents had shown up at her office. Brushing aside the objections of the senior management and their protestations about freedom of the press, the agents had presented a subpoena that allowed them to remove all of her research notes on the article she'd written about the mysterious circumstances surrounding supposedly deceased military and law enforcement personnel.

Standing in her senior editor's office, arms crossed and one toe tapping, Siobahn demanded, "Why does the FBI need my notes now on an article that has already run?" What she really wanted to know was why the FBI had waited so long to take action. Surely they'd discovered the same information she'd published. That men from the FBI, other law enforcement agencies, and the military had been reported as dead, then later reappeared, alive, hundreds or thousands of miles away from their last known location. The men had all been more muscular than before, suggesting an excessive use of steroids. A few of them had been spotted "Throwing things around and roaring like damn Godzilla" per one eyewitness.

Not long after, most of those enhanced men had been dead. For real.

Yet during Siobahn's research she'd found no evidence that the FBI or any of the other affected agencies had been working to put an end to the situation. Although, Toby Andrews, an officer with military intelligence and the brother of her friend and former colleague Faith Andrews, had started an unofficial investigation into the matter. Unfortunately, Toby had then disappeared. Unable to find her brother, Faith had turned to Siobahn for help, fearing that Toby had suffered the same fate as the men in Siobahn's article.

With typical stoniness, Ajax Fairchild, the jerk of an agent-in-charge—yes, dammit, another ex, although at least she hadn't married this one—refused to answer. "Sorry, we can't tell you that. National security."

"Where were you three months ago when my story ran?" she countered. "Don't you think the FBI should have taken action to protect its agents long before now?" Oops. Seemed she wasn't going to hold back after all.

But Ajax—who the hell named their son Ajax in this day

and age? Even worse, what did it say about her that she'd slept with him despite his overblown name?—ignored her question. After his team boxed up her paper files, the small whiteboard she hadn't erased because she'd been working on a follow-up article, and confiscated her computer, Ajax handed her a form. "Sign this, please."

She felt so smug as she scrawled her name, acknowledging that the FBI had given her a receipt for the removed items and swearing that there were no other items on the premises covered by the FBI's subpoena.

Her smugness lasted until Ajax pointed out that the subpoena covered any information she kept at home, as well. Angry at the violation of her privacy when she hadn't done anything wrong, and wary because it was likely people within the FBI had been part of the cover-up, she insisted on being present, along with the newspaper's lawyer, while the FBI entered the premises.

It wasn't the first time she'd ended up on the wrong side of government scrutiny because of a story she'd been chasing. Just never before inside the United States.

Of course, this was also the first time she'd uncovered such a far-reaching conspiracy within her own government. She had evidence suggesting that the missing men had been forced into a secret government program run by a man named Dr. Kaufmann. In pursuit of their goal of creating superhuman soldiers, Kaufmann's scientists treated their subjects as disposable tools without regard to the men's consent, comfort, or survival. The program operated under such a high level of secrecy that some extremely powerful government officials had to be involved in covering up its activities.

In fact, Siobahn believed the conspiracy reached all the way to the Oval Office. A little over two months ago, Faith had called Siobahn and warned her to drop her investigation into the disappearance of Faith's brother Toby. Faith had learned that

President Bryne MacAdam planned to use Kaufmann's enhanced soldiers in an unspecified upcoming attack.

The President's involvement explained why Siobahn's contacts had shut the door on her inquiries, but it drove her crazy that she'd failed to ferret out the details. All she'd had were Faith's reassurances that capable people were working to stop the attack.

Then, several weeks later, President MacAdam had mysteriously resigned. The animated politician who'd loved to talk to the public in person had read a prepared statement from an undisclosed location, wearing a fixed expression that would have done Stonehenge proud.

The short speech had included an unconvincing line about him still being unable to come to terms with his son's death five years ago at the hands of terrorists. Since his resignation had occurred shortly after the anniversary of the day his son died, the statement had been taken at face value by the press.

Except, nope, Siobahn hadn't bought it.

While she didn't have any direct evidence—only Faith's statement about the President's involvement—Siobahn had pieced together a story she believed was closer to the truth. President MacAdam had decided to destroy some unnamed target in retaliation for the death of his son five years ago. He'd planned to use Kaufmann's enhanced soldiers, including Faith's brother Toby, to carry out the attack. Then some unknown group had stopped the attack and forced MacAdam to resign.

As if to prove her theory, once the President resigned Siobahn's contacts started talking to her again. Suspicious? No, not all.

Uh-huh. Ri-ight.

Unfortunately, her contacts didn't have anything more to add to what she'd already discovered.

Then, a month ago, the news had broken—her paper had been scooped by their main rival, damn it—that MacAdam had died of an apparent heart attack. While her newspaper's White House correspondent had handled the immediate coverage, Siobahn had gone to her editor and received approval to include the former president's death in her follow-up investigation regarding the missing law enforcement and military personnel.

She found the timing of his death suspicious.

Treading carefully, because if she was right and MacAdam had been murdered Siobahn didn't want to draw unwanted attention to herself and risk physical harm, she'd begun mining her contacts for information regarding the former president. So far, she hadn't received any responses beyond the expected expressions of sorrow over his death.

But apparently she hadn't been careful enough, if the FBI had suddenly decided she was worth investigating.

What Siobahn didn't know was whether this FBI raid was a result of high-ranking government officials covering their tracks, or a genuine effort by the FBI to finally investigate what had happened to their men. Either way, it was a good thing she only performed innocuous household tasks on her home desktop, such as paying bills and emailing friends. The personal laptop where she kept the majority of her research was currently locked in a safe deposit vault in Baltimore.

After the FBI's team finished with her home, Ajax asked her to accompany them down to headquarters for questioning. If it had been anyone else but Ajax asking, Siobahn would have refused, remembering Faith's warning.

"Please," Faith had said. "Don't draw any attention to yourself, Siobahn. I mean it. Lock your notes away so no one suspects you've kept them. Then focus on other things. A lot of very powerful people are running scared right now. Until they're all rounded up, you're in danger of being killed."

Siobahn had scoffed at that.

"I'm serious, Siobahn. I can't tell you what I know because

I'm under oath not to talk about it, but the people who hid Kaufmann's program will not hesitate to kill you if they think you're a threat."

Even if others at the FBI couldn't be trusted, Siobahn knew that Ajax was an honest man and would do his best to protect her. So she'd agreed to go with him to FBI headquarters.

Now Siobahn and the newspaper's lawyer sat across from Ajax in a small room while he interrogated her regarding her investigation.

"Give me the name of your sources regarding the missing men, Siobahn," Ajax said as casually as if they were out on a date and trading mundane details about their day.

"No comment."

"You know my client can't answer that question," her lawyer added.

"Who else did you talk to about your investigation?"

"No comment." Ajax understood enough about journalism to know that Siobahn had talked to her editor about her original article. If he didn't also know that Siobahn had been helping Faith to find Toby, which involved sharing her notes, then Siobahn wasn't going to enlighten him.

"Does the name Kerberos mean anything to you?" Ajax asked.

Siobahn hid her surprise. Damn straight she recognized the name. When she and Faith had started inquiring about a CIA black ops group called Kerberos that possibly had ties to the missing men, their research had hit a wall. For the first time in her life, Siobahn couldn't get people to talk to her. She'd investigated many sensitive topics before. Dug up dirt on people who thought they'd scrubbed clean all traces of their misdeeds. But not even her most skilled cajoling moved her contacts past their fear regarding Kerberos. People saw her coming and ran. Faith's contacts also refused to talk.

Surfing the Internet, even delving into little-known forums

about supposed government conspiracies had yielded nothing. Although they couldn't provide sufficient verification, Faith and Siobahn believed that Kerberos had funded Kaufmann's lab and used the enhanced soldiers for special missions, such as the President's anniversary demonstration.

"No comment," she finally replied. Given the secrecy around Kerberos, she wondered if Ajax had permission to drop the name, or if he'd done it to startle a reaction out of her. He should know better. Neither Siobahn or Faith broke under pressure. They wouldn't have survived years of overseas assignments in the war-torn countries of the world without being tough.

As if reading her mind—a trait Ajax had definitely not displayed during their short affair, thank heavens—he asked, "Are you aware that your former colleague Faith Andrews had been conducting similar research? And that her house burned down?"

"I saw the news report of the fire." Afterward, Faith had told Siobahn to stop investigating. She'd pointed out that if the men involved with her brother's disappearance had no compunction in burning down her house, they wouldn't hesitate to hurt Siobahn as well. Even worse, Faith feared for Toby's life if the men felt too threatened.

Which, of course, had only made Siobahn more determined to get to the truth. But in order to prevent any retaliation against Toby, she'd reluctantly agreed to temporarily halt her research. In the privacy of her own home, however, Siobahn had written up her notes and documented a variety of theories, making certain she'd be prepared to restart her investigation as soon as it was safe.

And she'd kept her ears open for any relevant pieces of information.

None of which she intended to share with the FBI.

Ajax's questions went on and on, often asking for the same

information but in a slightly different manner. Yet Siobahn didn't dare tell Ajax the truth, even if she'd wanted to.

Not that the uptight agent would ever dream of breaking or even slightly bending the law, but who knew if one of the guilty parties had access to his files.

"For the last time," Siobahn said. "No comment."

Ajax leaned forward. "Dammit, Siobahn. I'm trying to protect you, here!"

She rolled her eyes. "Right. Sure looks that way from here."

"Siobahn—"

She put her lips to his ear. "If you're really determined to help, you should think about who among your colleagues you'd trust with my life."

His eyes widened as he sat back. Yeah, they might be completely incompatible even as friends, but the guy wasn't stupid. He knew she was implying someone in his agency was involved.

Ten minutes later, she was free. Siobahn bid a cheerful good-bye to her lawyer and headed to her favorite restaurant to wind down.

Poor Ajax. The FBI's raid had only reignited her determination to write that follow-up article. She was damn sick of everyone trying to muzzle her. Even Faith.

After Toby had been rescued, Faith had made Siobahn promise not to write that follow-up article. "Toby and the other survivors of Kaufmann's program don't need their story making the news," Faith had said, the pain in her voice touching Siobahn's soft spot. "They're struggling to regain their humanity. It's not something that should be splashed across the front page. So please, let it go."

"You know I can't do that. I'll hold off on the article for now, but I need to know when it's okay to pick up the story again."

Faith's unhappy inhale had been audible. "I don't know if that will be...advisable."

Siobahn's ears had perked up. Advisable was their code for a story that was too hot at the moment, but would be exposé material once things changed. She'd understood that Faith would give her permission to proceed once it was safe.

With that in mind, Siobahn had made the promise to drop her investigation. And meant it.

Well, the FBI had just pushed her out of her play-nice zone. Their raid came too soon after MacAdam's death to be coincidence. Forget subtlety. It was time to bust some balls.

She dialed a number. When no one picked up, she left a message. "Faith, darling, you and I need to talk. The rules of the game have changed. Your grace period is over. You need to tell me what you know about MacAdam's ties to Kerberos. Call me."

DAMMIT, she was late again. Two days after the FBI questioned her, Siobahn re-clipped her press pass to her blouse's front pocket, picked up her purse from the metal detector's scanner, and waved good-bye to the guard as she slung the heavy bag over her shoulder.

"Henry, tell your brother he still owes me twenty bucks!" she called to the guard standing by the elevators. Henry gave her a grin and a thumbs up as she hurried past on her way to the staircase. His wolf whistle and "Nice legs, Murphy" made her roll her eyes, but secretly she was pleased. Hey, call her vain, but she had to admit that at forty-eight, she liked knowing her body was still considered attractive.

"Don't let your wife hear you say that, Henry," she called back as she hit the stairs at a pace dangerous to one less skilled in running in four-inch heels. Aware that her pace had hiked up her skirt to nearly indecent levels, she tried tugging it down once she was out of sight of the guards. *Damn you, Farsil. You owe me one.*

She hated covering Congress. Unfortunately, Farsil, another senior reporter at the newspaper, had finally taken a long overdue vacation with his family this week. Leaving Siobahn filling in on the Capitol beat. She'd done six months of legislative and White House reporting during her early years and hadn't been able to get out of the political morass fast enough. She'd rather be embedded with a military unit in a hot zone than forced to listen in on hours of boring testimony just to extract one interesting tidbit.

Of course, because Siobahn didn't want to be here, she'd left the office with little time to spare to get to the congressional hearing on climate change. Thanks to nearby construction detours, she was now late.

She barreled across the first landing, took a deep breath—damn, even with the amount of aerobic exercise she got every week she still didn't have the cardio stamina of her twenty-year-old self—and hurtled up the next flight. As she reached the top of the enclosed stairwell, a man turned toward the stairs from the corridor.

Siobahn collided with him and bounced back. One narrow heel slipped off the edge of the marble stair, throwing her off balance. She gave a little squeak of shock.

Strong hands caught her arms, steadying her and keeping her from falling down the stairs. Siobahn gasped and grabbed onto the man's forearms to anchor herself. He twisted slightly to the side, giving her enough room to get her feet underneath her on the slippery corridor floor while avoiding full body contact.

The man had moved so quickly, and held her with such strength, that Siobahn just blinked at him. Not many men—hell, none at all came to mind—would have gone out of their way to avoid plastering themselves against a female. Yet this man kept a polite distance between them, and his fingers didn't make any inappropriate side trips as he slowly released her.

For a moment she just stared in confusion at the suit covering a lean, runner's body. In her towering heels, she still came a few inches short of looking him in the eyes, which put him at slightly over six feet.

Six feet plus of considerate male who'd just backed up another couple of inches to give her more space. She looked up into his face, wondering who the hell had such good manners.

Whoa. The man's narrow, aristocratic face had the kind of enduring good looks that made women do double takes no matter what age group they fell into. His nutmeg brown hair showed silver at the temples. She'd heard other women say natural gray made a man more distinguished. Siobahn just found this man sexy. His mouth was a bit on the thin side, but she could work with that. She had the feeling that when he set his sights on a woman, he knew how to give her what she needed. Her nipples tightened just thinking about the possibilities.

She inhaled and caught the faintest scent of soap and aftershave. Nothing overpowering, which fit with his impeccable manners.

Most striking of all, his eyes were a pure, light gray. Almost silver. They gazed at her with an intensity that made her squirm and want to reveal all her secrets. Which would be totally embarrassing, given the way he made her think of hot, sweaty sex.

Hold on. What? Sex? Was she really thinking about sex *now*? In the middle of the freaking Capitol? She choked back a laugh. Well, at least her libido was alive and healthy. Given the recent drought in her love life, she'd been beginning to wonder.

Forcing her thoughts back onto the straight and narrow, Siobahn said, "Sorry. I should have been watching where I was go—" Remembering the committee hearing, she checked her watch and swore under her breath. "Thanks for keeping me from falling."

She flashed him a smile, took a firm grip on her purse, and sidestepped around him. Then she headed down the corridor at a fast walk. *Damn, damn, damn. The first interesting man I've met in months and I can't stay to flirt.*

"Siobahn, girl, you're still racing around like your tail is on fire. You nearly bowled poor Ryker right over."

Siobahn stopped, glancing over at a portly man with a shocking mop of thick gray curls beaming at her. "Hello, Uncle Sheldon." Sheldon Wallace, the senior senator from Pennsylvania, had grown up with her father and the two had remained close. Their families had spent so much time together when she was a kid that Siobahn and her brothers felt like part of the Wallace family.

"I thought you'd outgrown your recklessness, Siobahn." Wallace smiled to take the bite out of his words.

Used to his polished censorship of her behavior, Siobahn turned to look back at the man who still stood calmly where she'd left him, those piercing gray eyes making her shiver. She had the feeling that it would take more than one reporter in a hurry to unbalance the sexy Mr. Ryker.

She shot a grin at Wallace. "No harm, no foul," she countered. She moved in, accepted his bussed kiss across her cheek, then tapped her watch. "Climate change hearing. I'm late."

Wallace nodded. "Of course. But if you're going to make a habit of gracing our halls again, young lady, then I expect a chance to catch up with you over lunch."

"I'll set it up. I want to get a quote from you about the death of President MacAdam." With a jaunty wave, which she admitted was mostly for Ryker's benefit, she hurried down the hall, dodging a group of men filing out of a conference room. Wallace was one of the few congressmen she had any respect for. He might be old-fashioned in his attitudes towards women, but he wasn't creepy. He just thought women were special creatures who deserved pampering and that it was a man's privilege to smooth the way for the women in his life. He'd been highly opposed to her career as an investigative journalist, but then none of the males in her family had approved of her dangerous job, either.

Still, Wallace was one of those rare men whose word still meant something. She might sometimes disagree with his politics, but he always took time to listen and to examine his opponent's point of view before reaching a decision.

Forced to keep to a more sedate pace due to the slipperiness of the floor, Siobahn wondered who Ryker was. It had been a while since she'd closely followed the machinations inside the Capitol, but she knew he wasn't a congressman.

Besides, with that well-balanced posture and his quick reflexes, she'd peg him as military. Or, given that he looked to be in his early sixties and had been dressed in a high quality wool suit and not a uniform, more likely he was former military.

Too bad. She'd been married to a military man. Once had been enough.

Hold it right there, girl. Marriage? You just laid eyes on the man for the first time.

She'd have thought by now she'd have learned her lesson regarding being impulsive in matters of the heart. And, in fact, she hadn't had a serious relationship in... God, was it two years? Something that was unheard of for her. But then, becoming a team leader at the paper had kept her so busy between her own investigations and editing the team's pieces that she'd only had a few short-term lovers.

So what was it about Ryker and his penetrating gray eyes that intrigued her so much?

Spotting the door to the hearing up ahead, she buried all thoughts of romance, slipped her notebook and pen out of her oversized purse, and prepared to try and make a congressional hearing interesting for her readers.

CHAPTER TWO

"Watch out for that one," Senator Wallace told Ryker as he started down the stairs. "She's a reporter. I've known her since she was in diapers and she's always been tenacious. If she gets a scent of the reason you're here, she won't let go until she's uncovered the entire story."

Ryker nodded and joined the senator on his march to the lower level. He didn't bother pointing out that he'd noticed Siobahn Murphy's press pass. Or that he'd recognized her name. The Surgical Strike Unit, the privately run special operations group Ryker headed, had been keeping tabs on Ms. Murphy since the publication of her article about missing military and law enforcement personnel. After the Department of Defense and the FBI had failed to make any headway into locating their missing service members, they'd hired the SSU to investigate, so Ryker had been particularly interested in Ms. Murphy's conclusions.

At the time her article was printed, she'd hinted at a cover-up of the disappearances and suggested that the missing men had been funneled into an experimental government program attempting to create a super soldier. Although she'd given no names or other incriminating details, the SSU had continued to keep tabs on her.

"You're doing good work, boy," Wallace said when they reached the bottom of the stairs. He clapped Ryker on the shoulder once before striding out.

Ryker shook his head and shared an amused look with the guard. At seventy-six, Wallace called everyone under seventy "boy," but it was a word sixty-three-year-old Ryker didn't usually hear describing himself.

He turned in his visitor's pass and signed out of the logbook before following the senator into the bright D.C. sunshine. Slipping his sunglasses on his nose, he took the least crowded sidewalk away from the Capitol. His office was within walking distance and he needed the time to think. Not to mention that he preferred to check for a tail while on foot, rather than in the snarl of city traffic.

Several times lately he'd had the sixth sense of being watched, as he did right now. Listening to his instincts, he decided to take a circuitous route through the nearby streets. His current tension wasn't fully due to the invisible threat, however. He'd just come from a testy meeting of the joint House and Senate committees on intelligence, something that always left him edgy.

As expected, the congressmen had ranted and blustered about being kept in the dark regarding the ultra-black ops group Kerberos that Wayne Jamieson, the former Director of In-House Projects at the CIA, had been operating right under the CIA's noses. Because the SSU had been hired by the DOD and FBI to look into the reappearances of the supposedly dead service personnel, and because the SSU had made the connection between Kerberos and the missing men, Ryker had been stuck explaining to Congress that yes, Jamieson had authorized

Dr. Leonard Kaufmann to continue research into creating enhanced soldiers. Research that had started with Kaufmann's former boss, Dr. Mikhail Nevsky, during the Vietnam War.

Ryker had been the one to inform the congressmen that Jamieson had worked with contacts within other agencies to select candidates to be used as subjects by Dr. Kaufmann, then arranged for the men to be reported dead. After completing Kaufmann's program, the enhanced soldiers had been sent to Kerberos, at which point Jamieson sent them on illegal missions against the enemies of the United States.

Most recently, several of Kerberos's enhanced teams had been ordered by President MacAdam to murder thousands of innocents on a remote island in the South Pacific. The anniversary demonstration, as the President had hinted at a press conference earlier in the year, had been a matter of revenge. Five years ago, while MacAdam was serving as the ambassador to Indonesia, his five-year-old son had been murdered by unknown terrorists.

This year, MacAdam had finally received intelligence pinpointing the home villages of the terrorists. He'd made the decision to have assault teams put a deadly, slow-acting chemical into the water systems of the villages, then kill anyone who tried to escape.

While Ryker understood the agony of losing a child—he still felt the dull stab of grief over losing his wife and children thirty-two years ago—he couldn't condone the President's actions. Ryker and his special ops group in Vietnam had witnessed what devastating consequences the proposed chemical, Agent Styx, had on not only the targets, but the men assigned to dispersing it. With the help of his surviving friends from that special ops group —the FBI's Matt Jordaine, House Representative Brit Remington, General Aldrick Wehrig, and the CIA's Roger Brown—the SSU had stopped the attack and MacAdam had been arrested.

Then Stephen Cornelison, the newly instated President, had sworn everyone involved to secrecy. Not even Congress was to know the extent of MacAdam's treachery. Cornelison even insisted that everyone not directly involved be told that the President had resigned for personal reasons.

Keeping an eye on his surroundings, Ryker waited patiently for the walk signal by the National Gallery of Art to change. Withholding information from Congress bothered him, yet at the same time he understood Cornelison's position. The President didn't want to panic the nation unnecessarily. After all, the attack had been stopped. MacAdam had been removed from power.

"It's important that the running of the country continue as if nothing has happened," President Cornelison had insisted.

Ryker's protests had been ignored. Then, a month ago, MacAdam, Jamieson and Kaufmann had all died of alleged heart attacks. However, sources close to the events suggested that there had been such irregularities in the deaths that the blood and tissue samples had been sent to four different labs for analysis. Results were still pending, but Ryker's instincts were already screaming murder, particularly since several associates of Kaufmann and Jamieson had also died within the same time period.

Ryker knew that not all of the people involved with Kerberos, the anniversary demonstration, and Kaufmann's lab had yet been caught. In fact, it was likely that some of the people he'd faced across the table at today's meeting had known more than they'd let on.

Including his friends from Vietnam.

He hated thinking that one of the men he'd trusted with his life during the war could have ordered the murders, but he had to be smart. The only other people who knew the full extent of the situation were the Chief Justice of the Supreme Court,

President Cornelison, the White House legal counsel and the Secretary of State.

The Secret Service and FBI agents involved in the arrests knew part of the story, and might have suspected more, but all of the agents had been cleared of involvement with Jamieson before being given their assignments. Ryker didn't think the watcher he sensed was one of them.

The walk signal turned white and Ryker surged ahead with the rest of the afternoon crowd, searching for anyone moving too close or taking an undue interest in him. Given the nature of his current thoughts, it might be wise to use a bodyguard until this matter was resolved.

His gut told him the remaining conspirators were trying to cover their tracks. Putting in jeopardy everyone involved with investigating the matter.

Including the lovely Ms. Siobahn Murphy.

Faith had assured him that her former colleague had promised not to run any follow-up articles, and Ryker's research indicated Ms. Murphy appeared to be abiding by her promise. To his knowledge, none of the key players had recently mentioned the reporter's name. Which meant that she'd dropped safely off the radar.

Today, though, her luck had run out. Not only had Wallace warned Ryker about the danger if she found out what they'd been discussing, but Ms. Murphy had walked through the group of congressmen and security agency personnel still milling about after the conclusion of their meeting. Ryker had seen more than one speculative glance follow her. Given the classified nature of the situation, no one wanted a skilled reporter nosing around, and most of them would have heard her request that Wallace comment on MacAdam's death.

If one of the meeting's attendees had played a role in Kerberos's activities, then Ms. Murphy's life could be in danger.

Ryker knew that Siobahn Murphy had a reputation for tough, insightful journalism. She also showed a disregard for her own safety that probably drove her family and friends crazy. He understood such dedication. He'd often been accused of putting work before his own well-being, and many of his SSU agents operated the same way.

Having finally met her in person, it bothered him on a fundamental level that the vibrant redhead with the moss green eyes had come close several times to losing her life in pursuit of a story. His blood still hummed from their brief contact and he hoped he'd have the chance to see her again.

In the meantime, it wouldn't do any harm to assign a temporary, clandestine bodyguard to her.

Is putting a bodyguard on her a professional or a personal move?

Ryker suspected the answer was a combination of both.

He reached his office building and used his key card to open the front door. Nodding to the guard in the lobby, Ryker headed for the secure elevator. An attractive blonde got on one floor after him and gave him a flirtatious smile. But all Ryker could think about was thick red hair and laughing green eyes, so he gave the blonde a polite, impersonal dip of his head, then proceeded to ignore her.

Ms. Murphy intrigued him, packing so much life and energy into her five-foot-six, pinup girl body that the air practically sparked around her. He knew she was forty-eight, and he'd seen the fine lines around her eyes to prove it, but from a distance she appeared to be in her mid-thirties. With the toll the whole Kerberos affair had taken on his beliefs, not to mention the long hours he'd put in while trying to keep his people safe, Siobahn Murphy's vitality made him feel incredibly tired. And more than fifteen years her senior.

At the same time, the thought of seeing her again filled him with heady anticipation. He couldn't remember the last time he'd wanted to kiss a complete stranger just to see if she tasted as alive as she looked. To lean in and explore the complex, spicy scent of her.

Unfortunately, until the whole Kerberos fallout was cleaned up, he wouldn't have time to pursue the fascinating reporter.

"ARE you certain that none of the Kerberos employees who have been moved to other departments will talk?"

Myron Zybriesky bit back a sigh. The man on the other end of the phone line was using a scrambler to hide his voice and the resulting mechanical sound grated on his nerves. "Yes," he said. As much as he hated these conversations, this man with the disembodied voice was one of the main funders of Kerberos. Without his support, Myron would never be able to restart the program.

"Unfortunately," Myron said, "I've already approached all of my former colleagues. Only two of them expressed any interest in seeing Kerberos reborn."

"That's a pity. This country needs a program like Kerberos in order to stay great."

That right there was the reason Myron couldn't risk alienating this man. He was the only one so far who hadn't given up on the dream of the United States having a group of über-powerful soldiers able to carry out any actions necessary in order to maintain national security.

"I agree, sir," Myron said. "But as we've discussed before, when we restart the program we need to make certain everyone who signs up shares a certain level of commitment. We can't risk another traitor like Mark Tonelli."

"True, true."

Myron had initially resented Tonelli for his quick rise to a place of confidence by Jamieson's side. Then he'd learned that Tonelli had been responsible for revealing Kerberos's secrets to the SSU, which had led to the destruction of Kaufmann's lab and the dismantling of Kerberos. Now Myron wanted revenge against Tonelli. Unfortunately, the former agent had disappeared, no doubt being sheltered by the SSU.

"Have you found any sign of Jamieson's backup notes?" the voice asked.

"No, sir." Myron knew his former boss had been smart enough to keep extra copies of his data on the program, just as he was certain that Dr. Kaufmann would also have kept backup of his research.

With both Jamieson and Kaufmann dead, Myron had to find those backup notes or he'd never be able to resurrect the program. Unfortunately, he didn't have any contacts with access to data the SSU might have removed before they leveled Kaufmann's compound. "I can try to sneak into Jamieson's office and see if the FBI overlooked anything," he offered. He doubted the FBI would have been so careless, but at this point any action was worth a try. Without Kaufmann's data, Myron and his mysterious contact were just spinning in circles. "Do you have the ability to arrange for the release of the scientists who worked with Kaufmann?"

"I'm working on it."

Whether the scientists would know enough details to rebuild Kaufmann's program or whether the scientist had, like his boss Dr. Nevsky before him, kept his employees in the dark except for the small area of their individual responsibilities, Myron didn't know. He could only hope that someone would be able to piece together enough data to get a new lab up and running.

In the meantime, Jamieson's office, despite the yellow tape, beckoned. It wouldn't take much effort to get into the office undetected. Myron had a few ideas where to look for Jamieson's backup. Places the investigators might have overlooked.

The most important information he needed was a list of bank account numbers and instructions on how to access the money. The man on the other end of the phone line had already explained that with the government in chaos after the death of President MacAdam, not to mention the increased scrutiny of all areas of government while the Kerberos investigation was winding down, it would be impossible for him to send funds in the near future.

"Let me know if you find anything interesting in Jamieson's office," his contact said. "In the meantime, I'd like your help eliminating a few pesky loose ends. First on the list is reporter Siobahn Murphy."

Myron made a note of her name and five others who were deemed threats. "I'll do my best to find someone up to the task," he promised. "But with Kerberos dismantled, most of our agents are either in custody or have vanished."

"Hire a freelancer if necessary. Just make the problems go away."

"Yes, sir."

Myron stared into space after ending the call. He was mainly an analyst. Part of the administrative staff. He didn't have contact with the assassins and field agents. How then could he satisfy his contact's request?

Putting that dilemma aside for later consideration, he checked the clock on the wall. Good. It was late enough in the evening that there should be no foot traffic past Jamieson's office. He exited his office and found that indeed, the hallways were mainly deserted. Thankful that there were no security cameras in Jamieson's corridor, he used his key to open the door and then ducked under the yellow crime scene tape.

One glance told him his search was futile. All that remained were a few dust bunnies. Every piece of furniture and equipment had been taken away, including the carpet tacks. Gaping holes in the wall indicated where hidden safes had been torn free.

Myron quickly left the room and scurried through the deserted hallways until he came to the series of rooms that had been the heart of Kerberos.

Only to find the same emptiness.

Now what? He'd needed there to be an answer in one of these rooms. Instead, the utter thoroughness of the evidence removal was a clear sign that the FBI had no intention of allowing anyone to start Kerberos back up.

"What happened?"

The voice from the doorway startled Myron out of his thoughts. Turning around slowly, he saw a man wearing the office uniform of Kerberos's most recent team of enhanced assassins—a black nylon dress shirt with colored stripes at the collar, and black slacks.

Here, then, was the answer to one of his dilemmas. "The FBI has shut down Kerberos and stripped the office of anything that might contain potential evidence. Jamieson and Kaufmann are dead."

The assassin flinched. He was average height and weight, with thinning brown hair and intense brown eyes. He watched Myron with a focus that made him feel as if the man were cataloging a thousand different details about him. Or figuring out how best to kill him.

Myron shuddered, then sighed in relief when a moment later the man turned his attention to the empty room.

A somewhat lost expression flashed across the assassin's face. "I didn't know. I was out on a mission and just now returned."

He turned to look again at Myron. "What am I supposed to do now? Who will take my report? Who will give me my next order?"

"You're one of Kerberos's new assassins?" he asked, just to make certain who he was dealing with.

"Yes."

"Very good." A slow smile broke across Myron's face. "I'll take your report. And I have the perfect mission for you."

CHAPTER THREE

SIOBAHN TOOK a glass of wine off the server's tray and surveyed the well-dressed crowd at the invitation-only gala. Now that she was inside, the creepy feeling of being watched that she'd had ever since leaving home this evening had gone away. Some wine should relax her so that she wasn't jumping at shadows.

You're getting soft in your old age, girl.

No, she really wasn't. Years of war reporting had honed her instincts for danger. She'd been followed plenty of times in her life and knew the difference between benign surveillance and malevolence. Whoever had followed her here definitely gave off a threatening vibe.

Shaking off her nerves, she began working the crowd. Several of her contacts also attended this celebration of the reopening of the National Museum of War and Peace, but the man she'd arranged to meet hadn't shown up yet. She stifled a pang of worry. Maybe Lieutenant Brian Golding had changed his mind regarding passing on whatever information he'd considered so important that he insisted on meeting her in public. Or maybe he had a family emergency. Still, it wasn't like Brian not to call. And since he'd been one of her few contacts who'd actually seen some of Kaufmann's "freaky" soldiers in action, although at a distance, she really wanted to hear whatever new information he had for her.

She discreetly checked her phone. Nope. No message. She'd already left him a voicemail, sent him a text, and DM'd him on Twitter. It was his move now.

Since Faith also hadn't returned Siobahn's call, or her subsequent follow-up attempts, she had to wonder if word about the FBI raid had gotten out and scared her friends away.

Or maybe you're just overeager to get to the root of this story.

Sighing in impatience, Siobahn gave an approving glance to the pristine marble surrounding her. Not a trace remained of the extensive fire damage that a bomb had caused last year. Her newspaper had already run an article on the original incident. Tonight, another reporter was in charge of collecting data for a follow-up piece now that the renovations were complete.

Still, as Siobahn moved through the crowd exchanging pleasantries and small talk, she kept her ears open for any interesting tidbits. But only part of her mind was on tonight's gossip.

She couldn't stop thinking about Ryker, the man she'd run into at the Capitol. A satisfied smile curled her mouth. She took a sip of wine and praised herself for still having keen instincts. All during the congressional hearing she'd fought the niggling suspicion that the name Ryker should mean something to her. But for the life of her she hadn't been able to remember in what context she might have heard his name.

So on her way home to change for tonight's affair she'd stopped by the local bank where she kept a flash drive with her notes on the search for Faith's brother. Sure enough, she found a reference to Ryker in a summary of a phone conversation she'd held with Faith.

Siobahn had been listening to her friend beg her to end her investigation into the missing personnel.

"Ryk—" Faith had coughed quickly to cover her mistake. "I've been promised that the men involved will face justice, Siobahn."

Siobahn had made note of Faith's smooth cover-up of the name she'd almost let slip. At the time, she'd wondered who "Riek" was and why he was in a position to promise Faith justice.

After today, Siobahn was certain that Faith had been about to say Ryker, the spelling gleaned from his visitor's badge. But that was all she knew. Either the man was a ghost, or he had a team of computer experts erasing all mentions of his name, because her online searches had found absolutely nothing on the man. She didn't even know if Ryker was his first or last name.

Siobahn stared at the remaining wine in her glass. Her obsession with a man she'd seen for perhaps two minutes was ridiculous. Had she really looked Ryker up online hoping to determine what his role had been in helping Faith find her brother?

No, it had been pure feminine curiosity. Siobahn had simply wanted to learn about Ryker. What was his profession? Had he ever been married? Did he own a house? She'd looked for any data that would round out her impression of him.

Yet she'd found nothing.

She swirled the last bit of wine in her glass. Wariness warred with attraction, leaving her jittery. A man who didn't exist on the Internet aroused her suspicions. While Uncle Sheldon wouldn't have been so friendly toward Ryker if he operated on the wrong side of the law, Siobahn had enough contacts in the military and intelligence communities to know that some black ops work skated very close to the line between right and wrong.

If that was true, then a smart woman would give up now and leave the mysterious Mr. Ryker alone.

But every fiber of Siobahn's being rejected that idea. That in itself was probably a sign that she really should put him out of her mind. Yet she couldn't ignore the powerful reaction she'd had to his touch. The thought of never seeing him again was unacceptable, because...dammit, to get all sappy about it, she'd felt more than just a physical attraction to him. She wanted to explore his mind as well as his body.

Danger.

She shook her head, ignoring the too-late warning. The memory of the strength of Ryker's hands as he'd stopped her from falling morphed into a fantasy of what his touch would feel like on other parts of her body. Her nipples tightened and she gave thanks that between her molded cup bra and the beading across the front of her midnight blue cocktail dress, the proof of her body's arousal wasn't visible.

The corner of her mouth lifted. Well, at least she'd disproved the warnings that working too hard or being pre-menopausal would diminish her libido.

She'd almost made her way back to the refreshments table, when her father stepped into her path.

"Are you going to ignore me all night, Siobahn?" he asked gruffly, a teasing glint in his deep green eyes. Although he'd retired from the Army several years ago, tonight he wore his full dress uniform.

Careful of her wine glass, Siobahn gave him a one-armed hug. "Of course not, Dad. But you were having such an animated discussion with Admiral Gregg that I didn't want to interrupt."

"Hmph. I always have time for my only daughter. So, I suppose you're working tonight?"

"You know me, I'm always working."

"That's what worries me. Your mother and I—"

Siobahn rolled her eyes. "Dad, don't start tonight, okay?"

"You know we only want what's best for you."

Recognizing that her father was about to get started on one of his favorite topics, Siobahn blurted, "What do you know about a man called Ryker?"

"Ryker." Her dad's eyes narrowed. "Just what are you involved in now, Little Sib?"

Her lips curled ruefully at the childhood nickname. It really was true. In the eyes of your parents, you never completely grew up.

"So you know who Ryker is? I can't find any information about him on the Internet."

"Did you stop to think that there might be a reason for that?"

"Listen, Dad, I ran into him at the Capitol today. He was with Uncle Sheldon, so I'm sure Ryker isn't some major criminal. I just..." Hell. Did she admit she was interested in the man in a romantic way, earning another one of her father's lectures about throwing her heart after every intriguing man she met, or did she indicate that she'd heard his name in regards to an investigation?

Since she didn't know what danger might still be clinging to the facts surrounding Toby's disappearance—Faith had refused to tell Siobahn the full story—she decided to go with the instant attraction.

But her father hadn't made it to four-star general without knowing how to read people. "Ryker isn't a candidate for another one of your short-term crushes, Siobahn. He's a good man."

She bristled at the implication that she dated bad men. Okay, they weren't always the most suitable for long-term relationships, but that's one of the reasons she chose them. She'd never dated a crook or an abuser. Just men looking for a good time. Which, she had to admit, did not seem likely to be Ryker's style. His quiet intensity made her think he was an all-or-nothing man.

Another reason why she should run far and fast. Instead, she asked, "Is he married?"

Oh, way to go. Pumping Dad for information on a possible lover.

There was a startled pause while her father struggled with his surprise and when he spoke, his voice sounded strangled. "Um, as far as I know he's not married. But sweetheart, he's got to be at least fifteen years older than you. Once a man passes sixty, his body...uh..."

If the conversation wasn't so horrifyingly embarrassing, she'd have chuckled over her father's discomfort. Besides, remembering the feel of Ryker's well-muscled forearms underneath her fingers and the easy way he'd stayed balanced on the stair with the grace of a martial artist, she figured Ryker was in exceptional shape for his age.

Not that she'd criticize him if he did need Viagra, but...

God. Will you listen to yourself? Stop it, already. You don't even have any way to contact him should you decide to ask him out.

Feeling as awkward and as hormonal as a teenager, Siobahn swapped her empty wine glass for a full one off the waiter's tray. "Dad, just tell me if there's anything wrong with Ryker's character."

"What? No? He's one of the most honorable men I've ever known. Of course, I don't know what types of covert assignments the government sent him and his team on during Vietnam, but he runs that organization of his on a strict moral code. The country is safer for having Ryker doing the work he's doing."

"What organization?"

"Oh no, you don't," her father chided. "I'm not going to be your source for information on Ryker. If you want to find out what he does for a living, you'll have to ask the man yourself."

Un-believable. Her seventy-five-year-old father still managed to talk without giving away any information she could use to track Ryker down. Apparently she'd been naïve to think that retirement made her father the easiest target in the family for getting the lowdown on Ryker. Lord knew her four brothers with their various military and national security jobs would keep tight lips on anything she'd find of value.

Thank goodness none of them were here tonight. After the way her father had picked up on her personal interest in Ryker, she didn't dare mention the man's name to her brothers. Not unless she wanted to be teased until eternity about not being able to stay away from military men, despite her vow never to date one again.

She sighed. At least her father had confirmed that Ryker was one of the good guys. "Never mind, Dad. Forget I asked."

"Yes, well, under other circumstances I'd say he'd make a good match for you, Siobahn. He's the steadfast type who would never let you down. But I hear he's even more of a workaholic than you. He'd have to be, with everything he's forced to deal with. Besides, the age difference isn't trivial." Her father cleared his throat. "If you're looking to settle down, I'm sure your brothers and I can find you someone closer to your own age."

And this was why she didn't call every day. Her father was even worse than her mother with the "Siobahn, you should settle down with a nice man and stop poking into other people's business" routine.

"No, thanks, Dad. I prefer to do my own looking. I just found Ryker fascinating, that's all." She paused. "Can you at least tell me if Ryker is his first or his last name?"

"Both. As far as I know, everyone just refers to him as Ryker. You know, kind of like that Sting fellow. If Ryker has another name, I've never heard it."

Siobahn rolled her eyes. Figured. The man just had to present the type of complicated, multi-layer puzzle that she adored. To only go by one name, there must be one hell of a story involved. "Ah. Okay."

Luckily, they were interrupted by one of her father's friends, another retired general. After a few minutes, the general wandered off and Siobahn started toward the refreshments table.

Her father followed her. "When are you next coming over, Little Sib? Your mother's in another one of her baking phases and you know I can't eat all of those cakes and pies."

Siobahn laughed. "Stop complaining, Dad. I happen to know that all your daughters-in-law will gladly take the baked goods off your hands." All her brothers except the youngest were married. To their collective dismay, none of their wives could cook beyond the basics. But that's what they got for marrying career-oriented women who chose to focus their energies outside of the kitchen.

Siobahn and her father filled plates, then chatted with more family friends. Eventually, though, her father kissed her good-bye and went off to speak with some of his military buddies. Siobahn glanced at her watch. It was late enough to safely say that Brian wasn't going to show.

After setting down the half-full glass of sparkling water she'd been sipping, she said her farewells. Then she went over to the guard standing at the station just inside the front door. "Would you please call me a cab?"

"Leaving so soon?" a voice said behind her.

Siobahn shrieked and spun around. The quick move caused her to lose her balance on her stilettos. Once again, she found herself being steadied by Ryker's strong hands.

"I'm sorry. I didn't mean to frighten you."

She gave a shaky laugh. "Guess the wine didn't calm my nerves as much as I'd hoped." Her heart beat a panicked rhythm and she wondered if Ryker could feel her accelerated pulse through his grip on her arms.

As soon as she had the thought, he released her. Siobahn shivered, mourning the loss of his touch.

"It is a bit chilly out here." He offered her a warm smile. "Can I convince you to rejoin the party while you wait for your cab?"

"It will be about fifteen or twenty minutes, Ms. Murphy," the guard said. "I'll come get you when it's here."

"Okay. Thank you."

Greedy to touch him again, Siobahn slipped her arm through Ryker's. "Did you just arrive? I didn't see you earlier."

"Why Ms. Murphy, were you watching for me?"

"No, of course not." Watching for him, no. Thinking about him, yes. She cleared her throat. "But, you know, we journalists are always paying attention to our surroundings."

"Which, of course, is why I was able to sneak up on you."

She grimaced, then shot him a look. "You did that on purpose. Admit it. You wanted to get back at me for nearly knocking you over this afternoon."

Ryker put his free hand over his heart. "Ms. Murphy, your lack of confidence in my gentlemanly conduct wounds me. I would never be so petty." Then he glanced down at her and his expression sobered. "I can feel how tense you are," he commented, stroking his fingers over her forearm. "Is something wrong?"

To her surprise, she discovered that she'd curled her fingers tightly into the sleeve of his suit coat. "Um..." *Oh, brilliant. Dazzle the man with your witty, intelligent conversation why don't you?*

Ryker stopped and turned toward her. "I know we've only just met, but if you're in some kind of trouble, I'd like to help."

"I—" She glanced toward the dark street visible through the glass panes of the front door. "This is probably going to sound crazy, but I believe I was followed here."

Great. This was so not how she'd pictured her next encounter with Ryker. A romantic dinner was more what she'd had in mind. Maybe some dancing. Not confessing to him that she didn't feel safe.

"No. It doesn't sound crazy. I've researched you, Ms. Murphy. Given your background, I expect you have excellent instincts when it comes to your personal safety." He paused, then looked over at the guard before meeting her eyes.

"Would you allow me to drive you home?" He nodded toward the door leading into the gala. "I can find at least half a dozen character witnesses in tonight's gathering if you need proof that you can trust me."

Her cheeks heated and she stared at her feet. "Yes, well, my father speaks quite highly of you."

Ryker's low chuckle had her raising her gaze. "Checking up on me? I'm flattered."

Her damn blush only grew hotter. "What can I say? Running into an attractive, mysterious man piqued my interest." The amusement in his eyes made her realize what she'd said. She opened her mouth to clarify, when he raised her hand to his mouth and placed a kiss on the back.

"I find you attractive too, Ms. Murphy. Now, about my offer to drive you home?"

"I—" She frowned. "Don't you have to make an appearance inside?" She nodded toward the gala.

"Yes, but my business should only take five, ten minutes tops. Would you be willing to wait?"

For more time alone with him? He had no idea how long she'd wait. Trying not to appear too eager, she said, "Of course. Thank you. I accept your offer of a lift home."

"Good." Ryker gave her hand another kiss, then they walked over to cancel her taxi request.

"Um," Siobahn said as she and Ryker approached the door to the event. She withdrew her arm from his. "It's not a good idea for us to walk in together. My father's already warned me away from you."

The flare of amusement in Ryker's eyes quickly turned to something hotter. He leaned down to whisper in her ear. "Do you always do what your father says? I find that hard to believe."

"No. Of course not. But unless you want to endure a lecture from him, we should walk in separately."

Ryker took her arm again and steered her firmly toward the door. "Ms. Murphy, you'll find I don't intimidate easily. I can handle your father." He crooked one brow. "Unless you'd rather not be seen with me?"

She squeezed his arm. "Don't be ridiculous. What woman wouldn't be proud to be with you?"

Despite her brave words, Siobahn was relieved that her father was nowhere to be seen. He must have left by the other exit while she'd been talking to Ryker.

True to his word, after leaving her at the nearly depleted refreshments table, Ryker returned within ten minutes. Then he escorted her outside and waited while the valet retrieved his car.

Siobahn shivered.

"Do you feel eyes on you?" Ryker asked.

She nodded.

"Don't worry, we won't be followed back to your place."

"Doesn't matter. I got the sensation of being watched as soon as I hit the sidewalk in front of my house. Whoever is spying on me knows where I live."

"Would you rather I take you to a hotel?"

She shook her head. "No. I refuse to be run out of my home by some amorphous feeling, no matter how uneasy it makes me. Besides, I have a state-of-the-art security system."

"All right. But let me put my contact information into your phone."

"Because?"

"Because it's faster for me to type it in than have me tell you while you type. And because I want you to call me if you sense further threats."

With a raised eyebrow, Siobahn dug into her purse and handed over her cell phone. Then she held out her hand. But Ryker just shook his head. "You're already in my contact list," he admitted.

"Oh really? Hmm... That was fast."

Ryker just shrugged and glanced down at her phone. But she thought she'd seen a hint of guilt in his eyes. That vulnerability made her decide that she was flattered rather than alarmed that Ryker already had her contact details.

To her surprise, Ryker typed his information into her phone with all the speed of a habitual texter. "I've entered both my personal cell phone number and my office number. Call me if you get scared," he said as he handed back her phone. "No matter what time of day or night."

Touched by his concern, Siobahn glanced down. Damn him. He'd put Ryker under the nickname field. So much for learning his full name. With a wry smile, she returned the phone to her purse, then wrapped her arms around her torso, wishing she could snuggle against Ryker instead. A few minutes later, the valet pulled a silver Lexus to a stop in front of them.

"Whatever work you do must pay well," she murmured as Ryker helped her into the leather-covered passenger seat.

"My job involves enough networking with the power players that I have to look like we're not constantly hurting for money."

"And are you? Always needing money?"

He smiled and shot her a look out of the corner of his eye before pulling out onto the empty street. "I think I'll save details about my job for our next encounter, Ms. Murphy."

"Siobahn, please. And are you so sure we're going to have a next encounter?"

"All right, then. Siobahn." Another one of those warm smiles that set her senses reeling. "Oh, we'll definitely meet again. I'd like to take you to dinner."

"I think I'd enjoy that." She laughed, giddy as a girl.

"Good. I'll contact you tomorrow to set it up."

Staying true to his word, Ryker took a long, random route through the city before pulling up before her house, which was only a few blocks from the busy heart of Georgetown.

Ryker escorted her up the concrete stairs leading to her front door, then waited patiently while she disabled the alarm.

"Well, I guess this is good-night," Siobahn said. Part of her wanted to invite him in, not ready yet to say good-bye, but she thought that might seem too forward. Maybe—

Ryker moved closer and cupped her shoulders in his hands. "I'm going to kiss you now, Siobahn."

Touched by his old-fashioned manners, she only had time to nod before his mouth covered hers.

Oh, God. Her hands gripped his forearms as the sheer pleasure of his kiss set her world spinning. The kiss was much more tender and respectful than she wanted, yet at the same time her blood ignited and she strained against his hold on her shoulders, wanting to move forward and press her body against his.

But Ryker stepped away from her. Those intense gray eyes now appeared to glow with desire. "I'd better stop before I lose my good intentions."

He backed up. "Remember, call me if you feel unsafe. No matter what time it is. Promise me."

"I promise."

"Thank you."

He turned and walked down the stairs with the grace of a well-trained fighter. Then stopped and looked up at her. "Close and lock the door. Now."

"Yes, sir!" Throwing him a mock salute, she followed his order. Leaning back against the closed door, a silly grin broke out on her face. Oh, yes, she was definitely going to see Ryker again.

She didn't move until the purr of the car's engine faded. Then she slowly made her way upstairs.

The grin stayed on her face until the moment she fell asleep.

"How'd it go on the Hill today?" Rafe Andros asked Ryker the next evening during their check-in call.

Bluetooth headset in place, Ryker stared out the window of his office, watching the last of the light fade beyond the Washington Monument and trying to fight off another bout of the melancholy that had been plaguing him recently.

"About how I expected," he answered. Having an office here in Washington, D.C. was a necessity in order to keep in touch with the government agencies that not only kept the SSU employed, but provided assistance with equipment as well. Yet lately Ryker had found himself missing the community of the SSU's Oregon compound, which was where Rafe was calling from. "A lot of blustering, but no one wants to take responsibility and everyone is scared that if they push too hard their name will suddenly be dragged into the open and linked to Kerberos." An even greater possibility with Siobahn Murphy hanging around. He found himself oddly reluctant to mention Faith's reporter friend, but Rafe would eventually hear what he'd done and it was always better to get the truth out in the open.

"Yesterday, I ran into Siobahn Murphy, Faith Andrews's former colleague at the newspaper." Ryker reached for the antique globe in the corner of his office and gave it a spin. "Until we've determined if the President's death was murder, and if so, who was behind it, there's still a real danger that the remaining members of Kerberos will clean up after themselves by eliminating anyone who might possess information on their illegal activities. In fact, Ms. Murphy expressed concern that she's being followed. So I've assigned a guard to her."

"Faith will be happy to hear that."

Ryker smiled. Rafe had been captured by Kaufmann and put through the enhanced soldier program ten weeks ahead of Faith's brother, Toby Andrews. Once Dr. Gabrielle Montague had restored Rafe to nearly his pre-capture self, he'd taken a special interest in the remaining victims. Along the way, he'd become friends with both Toby and Faith.

Not to mention falling in love with Gabby.

When the globe stopped, Ryker's finger hovered over South Africa. Hmm. He had a few good memories from Johannesburg, but hadn't really seen much of the rest of the country. He spun the globe again.

"How's Alexis doing?" Ryker had spoken to his designated successor before Rafe called, but he wanted another opinion. Rafe had been in training for the director position before his capture by Kaufmann, so he understood the complexities of running the SSU better than Alexis, who had only accepted the position recently.

"He's still working on being tactful," Rafe said. "But he's improving. I think he'll work out a lot better than I would have."

Ryker shook his head. "No, you would have settled into the role just like I did. I wasn't always the boring diplomat."

Rafe snorted. "Boring is the last thing any of us would call you, sir. I know several of the guys are still waiting for a rematch on the dojo mat so they can kick your ass."

Leave it to Rafe to dispel his somber mood. Ryker laughed. "Remind them that I have a few more decades of practice and that martial arts happens to be one field where youth isn't necessarily an advantage. How about Alexis? Does he participate?"

"Yeah. But he's still too wary about his new status. He's at the awkward phase where he doesn't know if he's an equal or a superior. The men kind of keep him at arm's length, not sure how to treat him. They'll work it out."

The unspoken truth was that Rafe should have been ready to step in part-time as Director of the SSU, but falling into Dr. Kaufmann's program had altered him too much. Gabby had reversed the worst of the side effects, but Rafe's mind still tended to process data at an extraordinary speed, giving him an occasional migraine.

Ryker had no doubt that Rafe could run the SSU even with the headaches, but in a job that required more diplomacy than aggression, the lingering rages that flared up out of nowhere disqualified him. True, the rages happened very rarely, and Rafe was getting better at taking himself away from others in order to work through the episodes safely, but neither of them wanted to risk Rafe scaring off a potential funder or one of the crucial political allies who advocated for the SSU within the halls of government. An even worse outcome involved Rafe's mental condition deteriorating to the point that he couldn't make rational decisions. While he and the other victims appeared stable now, no one knew what the long-term consequences of Dr. Kaufmann's drugs might be. If Rafe took over as director, then degenerated to the point where he decided to use the extensive firepower of the SSU in an irrational way, lives would be at risk.

So Ryker had put off his plans for retirement. Instead of transitioning out within the next year, he would remain as director for at least another three years.

This time the globe stopped with Ryker's finger over Antarctica, one of the few places he hadn't been. Hmm... Someday he'd like to rectify that.

"What's the report on your latest mission?" Ryker asked. Rafe and his team had been working with the DOD and the

FBI to track down the remaining Kerberos teams made up of enhanced men from Kaufmann's lab.

Rafe snorted. "False alarm, sir. Yeah, the men were bulked up a bit, but only through normal steroid use. Turns out their leader had heard about the enhanced Kerberos teams and thought he'd try to achieve similar results using high doses of regular steroids on his men. Idiot."

Ryker stared at the globe. As a former soldier, he knew all the ways a man could be worn down during war. Intellectually, he understood why leaders constantly strove to overcome these obstacles. But needing a good night's sleep, feeling pain, experiencing empathy—all of those were part of being human.

What Kaufmann had done to the men in his program had nearly erased their humanity. He gave thanks every day for the skills of Gabby, Kai Paterson, and the rest of the SSU's medical team for bringing Rafe and Toby back from that edge. "Any more prospects?"

"Yeah. We leave tonight." Ryker heard the weariness in Rafe's voice. "Enough time has passed that any men who went through the entire program will have deteriorated to the point of being dangerous."

"You have procedures in place for handling them?" Ryker asked.

"Of course."

Ryker knew it would hurt Rafe to put down a fellow victim of Kaufmann, no matter how violent the man's rage or how close the man was to complete organ malfunction.

That was the hidden truth that Jamieson had ignored and Kaufmann had tried desperately to change. After a month of torture and chemical injections to break the men's minds down while beefing up their bodies, Kaufmann's subjects only achieved four weeks at their optimal physical and mind control level. After that, their minds and bodies rapidly deteriorated. If the insanity and rages didn't drive them to kill themselves, their bodies quickly stopped working and they died from massive organ failure within three to four weeks.

"All right. Keep me updated." Ryker refrained from telling Rafe that he didn't have to do this. The younger man had made it his mission in life to save as many of Kaufmann's former subjects as possible.

"Will do, sir." With that, Rafe ended the call.

As Ryker stared at Antarctica's coastline on his globe, he realized he was jealous. Not just of Rafe's inner fire, which Ryker seemed to have lost recently, but because Rafe had Gabby in his life.

Giving the globe one last spin, he turned his back on it. Yes, he could admit it, he was jealous. Rafe had found Gabby. Rafe's brother Niko, also an SSU agent, had fallen in love with Jenna Paterson, the daughter of Ryker's murdered best friend. Jenna's brother Kai, who was going to head the SSU's new research facility into biochemical weapons, was engaged to Dr. Nevsky's daughter, archaeologist Susana Dias. Hell, even Mark Tonelli, the former CIA agent who'd once worked to bring down the SSU and now worked with them, had found his lady in Faith.

Is that why I'm so interested in Siobahn Murphy? Because I'm lonely?

Thinking about their kiss, Ryker knew that wasn't it. If he just wanted a companion, there were plenty of interested candidates, even at his age. Yesterday's blonde in the elevator being a prime example. No, it wasn't loneliness that pulled him toward Siobahn. Combustible chemistry, courage, and intelligence made Siobahn irresistible.

CHAPTER FOUR

"SORRY I DIDN'T SHOW at the gala the other night," Lieutenant Brian Golding said over the phone when he finally contacted Siobahn at her office two days after his no-show.

"You worried me, Brian," she chided.

"Sorry about that. Lizzy had a bad asthma attack and we spent the entire night at the hospital with our phones turned off. I shot you a quick text before we went radio silent, but never checked to make sure it got delivered."

"Is she okay?" Brian's six-year-old daughter had only recently developed severe asthma.

"Yeah, she's going to be fine. The doctor is trying her on some new medicine that should help."

"So, what was so important that you wanted to meet in person, Brian?"

"Remember how you asked me about those freaky soldiers a while back?" he asked.

Siobahn felt her eyebrows scrunch in surprise and knew she was adding to the lines that were starting to form on her forehead. Ah, well. "Yes. You clammed up tight just when I desperately needed all the information you could give me."

Now she suspected why Brian had gone silent about the strange soldiers he'd seen. He'd been afraid of retaliation from the top. He'd probably been afraid of suffering the same fate as Toby and all the other missing military men who'd been conscripted into Kerberos.

"Yeah, well," Brian said. "The silent treatment was as much for your own good as mine. You don't have any idea what the stakes were."

Oh, you'd be surprised. Given the amount of time she'd spent lately using disposable prepaid cell phones and skulking down deserted streets, she figured she was well on her way to earning an espionage merit badge. Yet until she determined who in the government had been involved in the cover-up, she couldn't afford to trust anyone. Not even the FBI. And wouldn't that just delight her brother Ian who worked for Homeland Security and was constantly engaged in a not-always-friendly rivalry with the FBI. Of course, since her family had no clue what she'd been working on, she couldn't very well tell Ian of her current predicament.

"So what's changed?" Siobahn asked. She rubbed her arms against a sudden chill and realized that the phone had gone silent. "Brian? You still with me?"

"Yeah. Sorry. Had to move to a more secure location. Listen, the reason I wouldn't talk to you was that we were under lockdown. On standby as backup for an ultra top secret mission in case something went bad. We were prohibited from talking to anyone on the outside."

"Is that usual?"

"For the entire base to be on alert like that? No. It's the type of situation you'd expect if an attack was pending. But none of us were aware of any situation that threatened to escalate into immediate aggression."

"Okay. So what's that got to do with why you're calling me now?"

"After the lockdown was over, I was having drinks with a buddy who works at one of the airbases. He said that during the lockdown a plane took off carrying a bunch of what looked like private soldiers. Some of them acted strange, similar to the behavior of the freaks we'd seen out at Ft. Bragg. Even weirder, there appeared to be several people in white lab coats who joined the group just before takeoff."

Kerberos's enhanced men. Had to be. "Exactly when was this? What was the plane's destination?"

"Uh, about ten weeks ago. My friend said that no one knows where the plane was headed." That was about the same time that Toby had been rescued and MacAdam had resigned.

"Why are you telling me this, Brian? If you're looking for the truth, you're in a better position to find it than me. You've got more access to the plane's crew than I do." Her investigative radar definitely felt something suspicious was going on. If Brian could give her details, then maybe she'd be able to tie the secret mission to MacAdam's resignation and death. But it didn't sound like her friend had much to tell her.

At this point, Siobahn figured her best bet for getting the information she needed was to see if one of her contacts could put her in touch with the team responsible for the security of MacAdam after his resignation.

"That's the problem, Siobahn," Brian said. "All records that the plane ever landed on base have been destroyed."

Figured. Siobahn sighed. "A cover-up is nothing new, Brian. You know I need more detail before I can investigate. Besides, I've been promised that the people responsible for creating the freaks have been stopped and will face justice." Not that she considered it justice that MacAdam had died before the public learned the truth about his sudden resignation. It stank of someone trying to cover their tracks.

Someone who might recently have turned his or her attention to Siobahn. Once again, from the moment she'd left the house this morning, she'd had the sense that someone was watching and following her. Sick of feeling afraid, she'd immediately called Ajax and demanded point blank if the FBI had agents tailing her.

"No." He'd actually sounded affronted. "Our orders were only to confiscate your files and question you."

Ajax might be a jerk, but he wasn't a liar. Which meant someone else was watching her.

Yet despite using all the tricks she'd learned from her over-protective, security-paranoid brothers, she hadn't been able to spot her tail.

It freaked her out.

Because someone ballsy enough to take out a former president wouldn't hesitate at eliminating one pesky reporter.

"Well, that's just the thing, Siobahn," Brian continued. "A few days ago, my team was out in the middle of the country in a remote forest doing some special maneuvers. The wind had changed on us last minute, so we were dropped several miles deeper into the forest than intended. That's where we ran into another one of those freaky teams."

"Wait. What? I—" She thought back. Faith had said that the people involved had been stopped, but nothing about whether all of the victims had been rounded up. Siobahn swore under her breath. "Tell me everything, Brian."

"There's not much to tell. At first, we only knew these weren't regular soldiers because of the unique black uniforms they wore. Colored stripes decorated their left shoulders in a ranking system I've never seen before. All of the men were huge. Like they'd been taking massive doses of steroids. We took up observation positions in the woods and they never noticed us. A few of us snapped photos. I'll send them to you."

Siobahn did a fist pump, glad that her door was closed so her colleagues couldn't see her elation.

"Then, as the men moved out of sight," Brian continued,

"we noticed that some of them were weaving slightly on their feet and tripping frequently."

"Were they drunk? Wounded?"

"If it was one or two guys, I'd go with drunk. But out of two dozen men, I'd say at least eight had some difficulty moving. And if they were injured, their teammates should have been watching in order to step in and offer assistance if needed. Instead, none of the others paid the struggling men any attention. In fact, the team lacked the overall sense of cohesion and interpersonal awareness you'd normally see in a group that has trained together extensively."

"Is that it?"

"No. Some of us decided it would be a good test of our skills to follow them. Siobahn, they returned to a small compound built against the base of a hill. It almost blended in with the rocks and the trees. We might have missed it if we hadn't been paying attention. The place was surrounded by fencing tipped with razor wire and guarded by more men in black uniforms. I recognized one of the guards at the gate. He'd been recently deployed to Iraq but was reported killed by a roadside bomb his first week there."

Siobahn's blood hummed. "Did you report what you'd found?"

"Not yet. The guys want to think some more about the possible repercussions. They're afraid of what might happen to our team if it turns out people higher up in our command structure knew about the compound."

Siobahn bit her lip. "Brian, is there any suspicion that the ones responsible for covering up the existence of the freaky soldiers might be outside of the military? In one of the other branches of government?"

"That's not something I can speculate on." Brian's crisp reply sounded too rehearsed. He was hiding something. But she knew better than to push him when he started sounding all official.

"All right," she said. "I'll send you an encryption program from my secure email box. Send me everything you've got. And for God's sake, Brian, be careful. I don't want to hear that you've suddenly turned up dead."

"You got it."

As Siobahn got ready to hang up, Ryker's face popped into her mind. "Totally off topic, but I ran into a guy named Ryker yesterday. What do you know about him?"

"Ryker? You mean your dad and brothers haven't mentioned him? Really? He's something of a legend. Belonged to an ultra-hush-hush spec ops group during the Vietnam War. Stayed in spec ops after the war until he had a falling out with the powers that be. Left to start his own privately run special operations group, The Surgical Strike Unit, SSU for short. He's the commander everyone wanted to serve under. Tough but fair. Still has a reputation of being fiercely protective of the men and women who serve with him. A friend of mine joined the SSU and has been after me to follow him. But they're head-quartered in Oregon and my kids are in good schools here in Maryland, so I'm not ready to make a move just yet."

Siobahn's heart sank. Oregon. Figured a man as mysterious as Ryker would live out in the middle of nowhere. Well, no point in having regrets. They had a dinner date in two days and she'd enjoy his company for as long as he was in town.

"Thanks, Brian. I look forward to getting your photos. And once things have calmed down, I'll take you to lunch."

"Offer instead to babysit the kids so Samantha and I can have a date night, and I'll be in your debt forever."

Siobahn laughed. "Done."

"FAITH, before you remind me of my promise to let this investigation lapse, I've got to tell you that something new has come up. Something that whoever helped you find Toby is going to want to hear." Siobahn suspected that Faith was reporting back to Ryker and the SSU, but figured it was Faith's responsibility to share that information with her first.

"Siobahn—"

Hearing the warning in her friend's voice, Siobahn rushed on. "There's a hidden compound in the woods in South Dakota with at least one team of those freaky soldiers that I think might belong to Kerberos."

Faith sucked in a breath loud enough for Siobahn to hear over the secure line. "You're right. That does change things. We thought..." Siobahn could picture Faith shaking her head, setting her unruly hair falling out of whatever attempt she'd made to contain it. "I'm going to have to make some calls. See who best to put in touch with you."

Yes.

"Tell me everything you know," Faith demanded.

Siobahn smiled. "Isn't that usually my line?"

Faith chuckled. "Yeah. Sorry."

"Don't be. And don't forget that there's still a job waiting for you if you want to come back." Faith had quit journalism after her sister shot their parents to death then turned the gun on herself. The need to focus on her remaining family had been the main reason Faith gave up her job, but Siobahn often wondered if the harsh treatment Faith and her family suffered at the hands of her fellow journalists had soured her on the profession as a whole. "I promise this is the last time I'll mention coming back to work for me."

"I appreciate your confidence in me, Siobahn, I really do. And you know I love you like a sister. But I don't think full-time journalism is in my future. I'm not sure what I'm going to do, but it partly depends on where Toby ends up. Now, give me everything you've got and I'll pass it on."

RYKER SANK BACK in his office chair. "Run that by me again." The call from Faith Andrews had caught him just as he was getting ready to head home for the night.

"According to Siobahn's contact," Faith recapped, "there's a small compound of what appear to be Kaufmann's men in the wilds of South Dakota."

Ryker let out a sigh. Beyond his window, the night sky glowed from the lights over the city and an occasional spotlight roamed across the sky. Half the time the SSU was like that spotlight, a thin beam of light in an increasingly dark world. Taking care of one crisis only to face another, more deadly situation the next day.

Rafe and his team had located several batches of enhanced men who had been sent out on missions by Jamieson and never checked back in, or whose missions hadn't been completed when Kerberos was dismantled. Yet there'd been nothing in the notes confiscated from Kerberos headquarters to suggest an offshoot to Kaufmann's lab.

On the other hand, everyone agreed that both Jamieson and Kaufmann had been paranoid men. Dr. Nevsky, Kaufmann's predecessor, had stored his backup notes on a microchip implanted in the abdomen of his daughter, Susana Dias. After Nevsky had triggered the self-destruct sequence that had burned down his lab and destroyed all of his research, there'd been an international manhunt for the microchip. Ryker suspected that Kaufmann and Jamieson would have chosen a much more accessible backup location.

Maybe they hadn't kept their backup at a secure storage site, but at another compound that mirrored Kaufmann's experiments. What better way to guarantee the program would continue than to already have a second lab running?

Not wanting to jump to conclusions, Ryker admitted that Siobahn's contact might have stumbled across a simple training camp for Kaufmann's men, a camp that had lost communication with its command center and therefore continued on as usual, waiting for new orders.

Ryker tilted his head toward the ceiling. He was going to have to send a team to investigate. With Rafe's imprisonment still weighing on him, he would make certain all members of the team were volunteers who fully understood what types of horrors they might witness.

"Thank you for passing this on, Faith."

"You're welcome, sir. I...ah...haven't told Siobahn about the SSU."

"That's good. I've recently run into Ms. Murphy and if I feel she needs to know of our connection, I'll tell her myself." He didn't like the idea of keeping Siobahn in the dark, but he wanted to keep her safe.

"In the meantime," he continued, "please warn Ms. Murphy again that it's too dangerous for her to continue to pursue this."

"I will, but I can tell you right now, it won't do any good. I already warned her off once. With this new information, her instincts are back on full alert. When Siobahn gets her teeth into a story, she doesn't let go."

"I figured as much. However, the people involved in protecting Kerberos's secrets have already killed. I don't want Ms. Murphy to become their next victim." Ryker didn't voice his deepest fear, that if someone was trying to continue Kaufmann's program, he or she might not choose to focus their research solely on men, the way Kaufmann had. Ryker would do everything in his power to stop Siobahn from becoming a victim of such experiments.

"Rafe tells me you've placed a guard on Siobahn," Faith

said. "Thank you. She might not consider it necessary, but I'll rest easier knowing that she's protected from the men who hurt Toby."

"You're welcome." After what Faith had just told him, Ryker suspected the stakes were higher than he'd believed. It was time to talk to Siobahn about entering protective custody.

He knew he was in trouble when the thought of seeing her again, even to give her unpleasant news, filled him with anticipation.

The REPORTER sure did keep odd hours. And move around a lot. The assassin had found it challenging to keep the woman in his sights today, even with her red hair. She walked fast and skillfully slipped between her fellow pedestrians, often leaving little room for him to follow without bumping into people.

For longer distances, she took the Metro. Which presented another set of challenges as he tried not to lose sight of her on the crowded platforms, then worked to stay unnoticed while standing a few feet away from her in the train car.

By itself, this job wasn't too difficult, and with Kerberos dismantled he was simply glad to have an assignment. All he had to do was follow Siobahn Murphy and then find a way to kidnap her. However, the other man who'd been tailing her was going to be a problem. He acted more like a bodyguard than a tail, but if so, Ms. Murphy didn't seem to know she was being guarded. Still, he couldn't risk taking the other man out until he understood who'd sent the guard to watch the woman. Eliminating a law enforcement officer or other security professional would bring nothing but trouble.

In the meantime, he had to take extra precautions to avoid being spotted.

The assassin's orders were to stay undetected and he had no choice but to obey. A small voice in the back of his head tried to warn him that his unswerving need to obey no matter what the threat to himself was wrong, but he didn't listen. He liked the security of being told what to do. He didn't want the responsibility of deciding what was right and what was wrong. Jamieson and Kaufmann had been strong leaders to follow and he'd been happy to carry out their commands. Whether this new boss would also provide him such security, he didn't know. All he knew was that his panic over learning that both Jamieson and Kaufmann were dead had been eased when the new man gave him these orders.

He didn't care if his target was a male or a female. As long as he was told that national security depended on his actions, he would obey.

His phone vibrated in his pocket.

Change of plans, the text message read. *Kill her. Make it look like an accident. Or suicide.*

A heady burst of adrenaline flooded his system. Kidnapping a target was interesting work, but stalking with the intent to kill truly made his heart pound with anticipation. This was what he'd been bred for.

"Rafe," Ryker said when he called the younger man to pass on the information Siobahn had discovered. "I'm not asking for you and your men to go in. Let another team handle it." He rubbed the back of his neck. "This isn't a matter of you facing down a few of Kaufmann's enhanced soldiers, then bringing them to Gabby for treatment. This—"

"Stop babying me, sir."

Ryker winced at the anger in Rafe's voice. "Rafe—"

"I understand that you're trying to protect me, sir, and I appreciate your concern. Trust me, I can handle the situation." Rafe gave a slightly bitter laugh, something he wouldn't have done pre-Kaufmann. "The shrinks will tell you I need to face what's inside that compound if I'm going to put what happened to me in the past."

That didn't make Ryker's decision any less difficult. It wasn't just Rafe's state of mind he worried about. Rafe might be the only member from the original SSU team who had survived being captured by Kaufmann, but his second team had witnessed the horrors of the lab during their assault on the compound.

Setting an example for his team, Rafe spoke openly about continuing to seek help with his nightmares and his occasional bouts of rage. As a result, about seventy percent of those who'd participated in the assault on Kaufmann's compound had sought at least one session with a counselor.

Ryker shook his head and eyed his reflection in the window. Hard as it might be, he had to trust that Rafe knew his own limits.

"I'm solid, sir. Really," Rafe said. "If I didn't think I could handle this, I'd tell you."

"I see some of my mind reading skills have rubbed off on you." Or maybe his age was catching up with him and he was becoming predictably cautious.

Thinking about his age made him scowl. He did not want to think of himself as too old for Siobahn Murphy. He wanted her to look at him and see a man she was interested in romantically, not an older authority figure.

"Naw, no mind reading," Rafe answered. "I just know you, sir. So, have the analysts found anything in Kaufmann or Jamieson's data to indicate there were other branches of the program?"

"No. You never heard Kaufmann mention other bases?"

"Right. He occasionally sent us on multi-day training excursions, but I don't remember any permanent structures. This base could be just a trial outpost or it might be a fully independent program."

The weariness that had been pressing down on Ryker for weeks gained another couple of pounds. He'd hoped that they'd found all of Kaufmann's remaining victims. "I'm going to put Gabby and Kai on standby until we get this issue resolved," he said. Dr. Gabrielle Montague and Kai Paterson headed the SSU medical and scientific team responsible for reversing the effects of Dr. Kaufmann's program.

"I understand, sir. Continuing our long distance relationship a bit longer won't kill me or Gabby."

Ryker grimaced over Rafe's choice of words. "I'm sorry." With Gabby working out of the lab in Georgia and Rafe based out of the Oregon compound, Ryker knew the couple had precious little time together.

"Don't be. We both sleep better at night knowing we're doing everything in our power to help Kaufmann's victims."

Never let it be said that he didn't understand a losing position. Ryker had to accept Rafe's decision, both regarding his own mental preparedness for investigating the compound, and the readiness of his team. "Okay, Rafe, you win. You and your team are officially assigned to check out this compound. Under the condition that all members of the team be volunteers. I don't want anyone going with you who isn't ready to handle the potential of seeing the same sorts of atrocities that they witnessed at Kaufmann's compound."

"You got it."

"If you determine that this compound is a fully functioning program, report back and we'll send a full assault team."

"Understood."

After Ryker ended the call, he continued to stare into space for several minutes. Rafe's courage humbled him.

Yet you're afraid to confront one sexy woman.

Shaking his head over his unexpected nerves, Ryker picked up the phone. It was time to bring Siobahn Murphy in.

CHAPTER FIVE

Siobahn knew the moment she stepped in her foyer that someone had been in her house. The eerie silence indicated that the alarm had been cut off and no lights came on when she flipped the switch to the overhead light. A sixth sense raised the hair on the back of her neck and she glanced around nervously.

Damn. Probably whoever had been here was long gone, but Siobahn wasn't taking any chances. She spun on her heel and reached inside her purse for her cell phone. Her other hand had just pushed open the unlocked door when a movement in the air behind her caused her heart rate to spike. She jerked to the side and looked back. The faint illumination from the streetlight revealed a man in a black ski mask moving toward her. Siobahn had a moment to recognize the square tip of the gun in his hand before she heard a zing.

Taser! Her mind screamed the warning an instant before the probes embedded themselves in her back and the powerful electric current sent her muscles into spasm. She fell across the doorway. Her head slammed against the concrete of her front step.

And the world went black.

"Ms. Murphy?"

A strong, broad hand gently shook Siobahn's shoulder. At least she thought that was her shoulder. She felt kind of disconnected from her body.

"Ms. Murphy, can you hear me?"

Yes, she could hear him. The masculine voice had the faintest hint of a Boston high-society accent and sounded vaguely familiar. Siobahn had an exceptional ear when it came to voices. Not just in recognizing them, but in hearing the subtle cues that indicated subtext the speaker might not be aware of. It was a skill that had frequently served her well as a journalist.

So why did this man's voice make her think of two bodies entwined, skin to sweaty skin, while the voice whispered words meant to arouse? Siobahn started to shake her head, wanting to dislodge the image, but even that slight movement caused pain to spike through her skull.

She groaned.

"Ms. Murphy, can you open your eyes? I need to determine how badly you've been hurt."

Given the speed at which the pain was drilling through her head, she thought opening her eyes sounded like a really bad idea. But her "I don't want to" came out as "Idonwanna" spoken with all the petulance of an injured child.

"The recovery team is two minutes out, sir," another voice interjected. "They have a medic on board."

"Thank you, Ethan," the sexy voice said.

Siobahn made a sound of approval. She could listen to this man talk all day. The way the smooth, deep voice fired up her libido should be illegal.

Hmm. How come she felt so disassociated from her body yet her sex drive was working overtime? Had she been drugged?

She must have asked that last question out loud, and this

time spoken clearly enough to be understood, because the man answered. "No, Ms. Murphy, you haven't been drugged. You were shot with a Taser."

"Umph. Don't like it. Hurts." And it did. The pain in her head joined forces with the man's comment about the Taser to yank Siobahn fully back into her body. All her muscles ached. Damn intruder.

The hand on her shoulder turned caressing. "I know you hurt, Ms. Murphy. Just lie still. When you fell, you hit your head on the edge of the concrete step outside your front door. Because your spine is twisted, I don't want to move you unless you can reassure me that you have full control and feeling in all of your limbs."

"Not Ms. Murphy," she said, aware that her words still had a slightly drunken slur to them. "Siobahn."

The man's hand stilled its caressing. Had her comment shocked him? Why? Needing to understand why a request for more familiarity would have such an effect on the man, Siobahn forced open her eyes.

"Ryker!"

He smiled. "Hello again."

Crap. The man's effect on her with her eyes closed had been too powerful for her peace of mind. With her eyes open, and the memory of their kiss heating her blood, he was devastating. Those amazing gray eyes now held only concern. His lean cheeks were darkened with after-five stubble sprinkled with several white hairs. But the biggest shock was that instead of an elegant suit, he wore a dark, snug, long-sleeved t-shirt and a well-worn pair of jeans.

He crouched beside her, causing the fabric of his jeans to pull tight against very interesting places on his well-muscled body. Dang. She didn't know many men in his age group—or hers, for that matter—who looked so good. And it certainly had been a long, long time since she'd had such a potent reaction to a man.

Too bad she was in no position to act on her attraction.

"Siobahn?" Ryker crooked his eyebrows and amusement stole into his eyes.

Uh-oh, busted. "Umm?"

"Can you feel your hands and feet?" He nodded toward the inside of the house. "We'd like to move you off your stoop and onto a more comfortable surface if you're not seriously hurt."

"Oh." For the first time she realized she lay on her left side halfway out her front door. The pain in her head radiated out from the point of contact with the edge of the top stair of her tiny concrete landing. She was twisted at the waist, with her head, shoulders and torso on the outside, her hips bridging the six-inch rise to the doorway, and her lower legs sprawled inside the foyer.

The porch light was off, giving her some privacy from nosy neighbors. But the sooner they got inside, the better. She had a tough girl reputation to uphold. Being caught in such a vulnerable position would set her back in the constant power struggle within the cutthroat news industry.

The man who'd spoken to Ryker earlier stood at the foot of the five stairs leading to the sidewalk. She noticed him straighten an instant before a black SUV pulled up to the curb.

Siobahn's breath hitched.

"Easy. They're friendlies," Ryker said, his hand tracing another soothing circle on her shoulder. "They have one of our medics with them."

Siobahn hated lying here. Hated the vulnerability. Hated that Ryker was seeing her as a victim instead of the strong, fearless woman she usually was. But the pain in her head prevented her from obeying her natural instinct to sit up. Instead, she carefully assessed her body by making small movements, until by the time that Ryker moved aside to let a dark skinned, stocky man with closely shaved hair take his place, Siobahn was reasonably certain that she hadn't suffered anything more serious than a concussion and sore muscles.

Much to her relief, Ryker didn't move far away. He positioned himself two stairs down with his face turned so he could still watch Siobahn while he spoke softly to the men in civilian clothes who'd arrived with the medic. A moment later, the team headed around the side of her house toward the gate into the backyard.

"All right, Ms. Murphy," the medic said, his voice surprisingly gentle for a man who looked like he could carry an unconscious, wounded soldier for miles. "My name is Colin Daniels. I'm the team's medic. I think you're okay to be moved. Do you want some help up?"

She started to shake her head, then yelped as the pain in her skull tripled. The night sky spun and she squeezed her eyes closed. For a few heartbeats she lost track of time, only regaining awareness when she felt strong arms slip between her torso and the concrete, while another pair slipped under her legs. A second later she was airborne. They'd been careful, but the movement still set her head screaming and she couldn't stop a moan from escaping.

"Easy, we've got you." Siobahn identified the voice at her ear as Ryker's. Once again she lost touch with reality, because the next thing she knew, she felt the softness of her bed underneath her. The effort it took to open her eyes worried her. She really must have whacked her head hard to put her out like that.

Finally, she managed to force her lids to lift. Ryker looked down at her, worry darkening his eyes. His hand stilled, then finished drawing the edge of her comforter up over her body. Siobahn snuggled under the cover. While she'd been out someone had removed her shoes, stockings, and suit jacket. She couldn't decide if she was horrified or thrilled that Ryker might have performed such an intimate task for her. Hmm... What would he do if she asked him to continue undressing her until she wore nothing but her skin?

"Welcome back, Ms. Murphy." Siobahn jerked her gaze away from Ryker and met the amused glance of the medic. Her cheeks heated. Had her thoughts really been that obvious?

"Er. Hello." Siobahn cleared her throat. "I guess I'm okay, huh?"

"Well, ma'am, the bad news is that you have a concussion," the medic said. "You have a laceration approximately an inch long on your forehead and the beginning of a sizable lump. I've stopped the bleeding and bandaged you up."

Siobahn raised her hand to her head and felt the familiar texture of a piece of gauze taped to the left side of her forehead.

"The good news is that the bone appears to be intact, at least as far as I can tell without an X-ray." Colin shared a look with Ryker. "Given the nature of the attack, the boss here doesn't want you in a hospital."

Siobahn shot a questioning glance at Ryker. "Your investigation has attracted dangerous attention, Ms. Murphy. As soon as Faith gave me the information you received regarding the South Dakota compound I called to warn you, but got no answer. We discovered your cell phone in your purse. Its battery had died."

"Ugh. Too busy. Forgot." Which would have been a problem when trying to call for help.

"Until we know who your enemies are, Ms. Murphy, it's safer for you to be under our protection."

"Your protection? Who do you mean?"

A smile touched Ryker's stern mouth. "What? I thought your father told you all about me."

"Not Dad," she grumbled. "He kept your secrets, damn him. But I have other sources." Siobahn bit her lip so she wouldn't whimper as the pounding in her head intensified. "Ryker, first name unknown. Spec ops legend. Director of the SSU." A glimpse of something like embarrassment crossed his face as she called him a legend, but it passed so quickly she didn't trust her judgment. She found it hard to believe anything could embarrass the calm Mr. Ryker.

"Is that who all these people are?" She cut her eyes toward the medic. "SSU employees?"

"Yes. Now, can you tell me what you saw when you stepped into the house, Ms. Murphy?"

She wanted him to call her Siobahn, but sensed that he deliberately used her formal name to put some distance between them in front of his employees.

Probably a smart idea. He'd be going back to Oregon soon. Leaving her behind.

But before he left, she fully intended to get to know Ryker on the most intimate level.

RYKER WATCHED Siobahn's face as she thought back to the attack. When she closed her eyes, he glanced over at Colin. The medic held up a packet of painkillers, set them on the bedside table, then let himself out of the room.

When after a couple of minutes Siobahn still hadn't opened her eyes, Ryker prodded, "Ms. Murphy?" He couldn't stop himself from thinking about her on a first name basis inside his head, but he would do everything in his power to keep a professional distance between them everywhere else.

"Sorry. Can't focus."

Ryker cursed inwardly. Her words were slurring again. Colin was right, she needed a hospital and to have her head X-rayed. But the security risk was real. The man who'd—

"I got home late," Siobahn finally said without opening her eyes. A crease appeared between her brows as she concentrated on enunciating clearly. "I'd walked down to a restaurant in

Georgetown for dinner so when I got home I came in through the front door. My gut instantly told me something was wrong. Also, the alarm was silent instead of giving its normal beep to indicate that the door had been opened." She let out a heavy sigh. "I turned to leave. Something made me look back. A man wearing a black ski mask—very clichéd—stood behind me, just barely illuminated by the light from the streetlamp. He tased me. I fell. Blacked out."

Her eyes opened and he read the question in them before she continued, "I woke up and you were there. How? Why? Who was that man? Was it a robbery?"

Ryker had to admire the way her inquisitive journalist's brain hadn't lost its ability to focus despite her concussion. "No, it doesn't look like a robbery, but you can tell us if anything is missing once you're stable enough to do a walk-through. We're still working on the identification of the intruder."

"Not much here to steal," she murmured. "Have better things to do than collect art. Don't care much about jewelry. And the FBI already confiscated my research both here and at the office."

Ryker felt a spurt of anger that his contacts at the agency hadn't informed him they'd moved in on Siobahn. "I don't know anything about the FBI's raid. But since the SSU has been working with them on this matter, I'll certainly find out why we weren't told about it. Did they get all your data?"

"'Course not. Too smart for that. Kept all my critical data on a secure laptop. Locked it in a safe deposit box when Faith told me to stop investigating a while back. Still there. Even put flash drive back. All safe."

She smirked. "Stupid agent Ajax didn't realize that. Never really knew me, did he? Just saw a pretty face." Her nose scrunched up. "Good in bed, but Lord, the man drove me nuts out of it. Rules, rules, rules. Don't know how we lasted three weeks. Shoulda dumped him after three hours."

Ryker coughed into his hand. Partly to hide his laugh over her spot-on assessment of uptight Special Agent Ajax Fairchild. Partly to hide the burst of jealousy he felt hearing Siobahn talk about her ex. He really hadn't needed to know her opinion of Fairchild's bedroom skills.

Ryker knew from the background check that she'd had a string of lovers in the law enforcement and military communities, including a marriage that ended in divorce. After the death of her ex-husband in Iraq, Siobahn had gone through a period of dating other journalists, academics and a couple of scientists. But none had lasted more than a few months and his research indicated no current lover.

Even though he had no business thinking about starting a relationship with Ms. Siobahn Murphy, Ryker had to admit to being relieved that she was single.

"Confession time," he said, pulling up the armchair from the other side of the bedside table. "I've had one of my men shadowing you since an hour after you nearly bowled me over at the Capitol. Ethan called me when he saw you fall. His replacement had just arrived to take the next shift and Tyler is the one who caught the intruder trying to escape over your back wall."

Ryker had expected outrage or at least indignation. Instead, her eyes softened. "Why?"

"The matter you investigated about the missing military and law enforcement personnel isn't over, Ms. Murphy. I was at the Capitol the day we met for a meeting to discuss the aftermath of the program being shut down. Until that point, you had stayed away from any place where the parties involved might be reminded that your article played a minor role in the beginning of the whole affair."

"Why is that dangerous?"

She likely suspected the truth. Given the nature of the man Tyler Lynch had captured, Ryker couldn't justify hiding the pieces of information that directly affected her. "We don't yet know if all of the men involved in the cover-up of Kerberos's activities have been identified and taken into custody. I hoped that assigning you a discreet bodyguard would be enough protection until the matter blows over."

Siobahn gave a very unladylike snort. "A bit high-handed of you, don't you think?"

Ryker shrugged. "If you've done your research, you'll know that I pride myself on protecting my people." Not that he'd been able to protect Rafe from falling prey to Dr. Kaufmann. Although Ryker knew there'd been nothing he could have done to stop it, the guilt continued to weigh on him. After all, it had been his order that sent Rafe and his team back to the compound that day.

"Am I one of your people, Mr. Ryker?" The smile Siobahn gave him shot straight to his groin.

Ignoring his body's reaction, Ryker nodded. "Yes." What he wouldn't mention was that Siobahn Murphy was rapidly coming to be one of the more important people in his life. He suspected it was a losing battle, but for as long as possible, he intended to fight this sense of fate bringing them together.

"And it's just Ryker," he added. "Not Mr. Ryker."

"Ah-ha! Progress."

He shook his head, amused by the triumph in her eyes.

"Why am I safer here, in the house that some stranger broke into, than in a hospital?" she asked.

"Your house and yard are small and private compared to the sprawling public hospital. That gives us better control over security. My team has already secured the perimeter. We've also fixed your alarm system. The man who broke in has been taken into custody." Let her think that he'd been turned over to the police. It was safer that way. "You're as secure here as we can make it."

In reality, the intruder had worn one of the Kerberos

uniforms, which made him potentially too dangerous to enter into the criminal justice system. So the SSU would hold him. For now.

What the SSU's analysts had only recently discovered, and very people knew yet, was that Kaufmann had also been playing with the intelligence side of the equation, continuing the second branch of Dr. Nevsky's research. The SSU had found records indicating that after surviving the first stages of Kaufmann's program, a special group of subjects had then been given drugs meant to increase their mental abilities instead of their physical strength. The intent had been to create improved spies and assassins.

Ryker suspected, based on the color of the stripes on the intruder's collar, that the man had come from the enhanced intelligence side of Kaufmann's program. After the intruder was interrogated regarding who'd sent him to follow and attack Siobahn, he'd be taken to the SSU's facility in Georgia. Gabby and her team would then check him for any unusual changes to his system.

If it did turn out that the man was part of the newly discovered branch of Kaufmann's program, then the SSU would have to broaden its search for his victims.

"Do you know what the intruder hoped to accomplish by tasing me?" Siobahn peered up at him through half-closed lids. If she knew how sexy she looked, how much he wanted to crawl into bed next to her and just hold her, would she be frightened? Or welcoming?

"No. The man is a professional. He carries no ID and hasn't spoken a word." Even when the SSU's men had threatened him.

Ryker wasn't going to tell Siobahn that there'd been a noose hanging from one of the beams in her kitchen, with a chair placed underneath. Apparently, her intruder had intended to knock her out with the Taser, then hang her so the cause of death would appear to be suicide. Thank God, Ryker had assigned a man to watch her. He only wished he'd told Ethan to be more proactive. "Ethan and I want to apologize for not protecting you better."

"Ethan? Oh, the man at the bottom of the stairs. He was the one assigned to follow me?"

Ryker nodded. "The SSU is stretched thin on resources at the moment. I thought it was more important to have a man tailing you rather than watching your home. We were lucky that Tyler arrived in time to catch the intruder." He met her eyes. "I should have explained that you had a bodyguard, then Ethan could have entered the house first to check for threats."

Siobahn gestured weakly with her hand. "Being harassed and even occasionally assaulted is an unfortunate risk in journalism. 'Specially overseas. It's not your fault. In fact, another woman might be angry with you for presuming to take on the job of guardian angel."

Her lips flattened. That, plus the pinched look around her eyes suggested she was still in considerable pain. "Colin left some pain pills for you," Ryker said. "Would you like one?"

After a moment of tense silence, she whispered, "I think I'd better say yes."

He wondered how much it had cost her to admit that. She struggled to raise her head off the pillow, so he moved in and supported her with his arm until she was half sitting, half resting against him. The warm, soft weight of her body against him felt natural, as if they'd sat this way a thousand times. Ignoring the warning bells that thought caused, he shook one of the pills into a tissue and handed it to her along with the glass of water Colin had put on the bedside table.

She grimaced as she swallowed the pill and gulped the water.

As he helped her settle with her back against the pillows,

Ryker asked, "Are you saying you're not angry that I assigned a bodyguard to you?"

"I have four brothers in the military or law enforcement and my dad is also retired military," Siobahn said. "He's a big fan of yours, by the way. Anyway, I gave up long ago trying to fight against the protective instincts of alpha males. There are easier battles I can fight in order to prove my independence."

"I've done some research of my own, Ms. Murphy. I don't expect you have to prove your independence to anyone who knows even a fraction of what I do. You've got quite the reputation for taking on difficult assignments and of talking your way into—and out of—some dangerous and tricky situations over the years." She was smart enough to know he'd have done a thorough background check on her the moment Faith revealed her name.

Yet her background photos failed to capture the sheer vitality of the woman. Siobahn Murphy was a pure Irish firebrand from her bright red hair to her green eyes to the faint scattering of freckles across her milky skin that gave her a younger appearance than her birth certificate stated. But it was the fierce spirit and questing intelligence shining from her eyes that attracted him even more than the beauty of her face and the sexy curves of her body. He hadn't felt this level of interest in a woman since Elaine died.

For the first time in the thirty-two years since their deaths, the pang he felt over the loss of his wife and children seemed like an unwelcome intrusion. It bothered him, the feeling that in this room, at this point of time, a special bond was forming between him and Siobahn. A bond that had hope stretching its wings inside him for the first time in decades. Hope that was still so new, so fragile, that he feared any outside interference would destroy it.

Since Siobahn's eyes had closed, he let himself rub his hand down his face. These romantic, poetic thoughts weren't typical of him. He was first and foremost a practical man. He'd had to be. One didn't survive as a soldier in the crucible of the Vietnam War by being soft.

Yet he'd have to admit that part of his recent melancholy had a great deal to do with finally wondering if there could be more to his life than just work. After all, he'd just watched three of the SSU's finest, toughest agents fall head over heels in love. Why couldn't something similar be in store for him?

Considering that after Elaine's death he'd vowed to never again subject a woman to the dangers of his career, it was something of a shock to realize that he was rethinking that vow now that Siobahn had entered his life. Even if she was no stranger to the darker side of humanity, that didn't mean Ryker wanted her in the sights of the type of men involved with Kaufmann's lab.

Yet, much as he wished differently, it was too late to hide Siobahn away from her enemies. And he suspected it might be too late for his heart, too. After all, he'd had no real reason to answer Ethan's call in person. His team knew what to do.

But the panic he'd felt at learning that Siobahn had been attacked had required him to come see for himself that she was safe.

Dangerous, dangerous waters. And a deadly time to find his attention splintered.

Still, he couldn't stop himself from watching her and longing for the freedom to get closer. Her breathing wasn't quite deep enough to indicate sleep, but her eyes were closed and he was grateful for the chance to observe her.

When several minutes had passed, Ryker finally roused himself. It was time to go. An instinct he couldn't control had him leaning forward and pressing a light kiss to her forehead. Siobahn's lips curled up in a smile. Reluctantly, he pulled back, but she opened her eyes and grabbed hold of his shirt.

"Stay," she murmured.

"Siob—Ms. Murphy, I don't think that's a good idea."

"Yes." She tugged lightly on his shirt. "You fascinate me, Ryker with no first name. I want to get to know you better. I want our date, dammit. Then I want to make love to you."

He opened his mouth, whether in shock or to protest, he didn't know. Before he could speak she released his shirt and placed her fingers across his lips. "Shh. I know. It's too soon. But I need you to hold me. Just for tonight."

If it had just been longing he saw when he met her gaze he could have resisted, no matter how powerfully he wanted to agree. But the hint of fear lingering there struck a chord in him. He suspected that she rarely showed such vulnerability to others. Particularly not to a man who was practically a stranger.

For an independent woman used to relying on no one, no longer feeling safe in her own home, her sanctuary, must be frightening. Worse still that she was injured and reliant on strangers for her care. Ryker knew that anger would eventually replace Siobahn's fear. But for tonight, she was vulnerable.

"Please," she said. "Hold me tonight?"

Unable to resist her or his own primitive need to feel her warm and alive beside him, he nodded. Then he sent a quick text to Ethan to let the other man know he was staying. As he removed his shoes and belt, a tiny voice warned him that his overwhelming need to take a moment of personal time indicated that he'd been pushing himself too hard. That he was close to burn out.

A truth he'd deal with later.

Taking extreme care not to jostle her too much, Ryker started to lower himself onto the bed on top of the comforter.

"No." She reached back and flipped the comforter down. "Get under the covers behind me."

He shook his head in bemusement as he obeyed.

Siobahn chuckled. "Not used to following orders, are you?"

"No," he admitted, moving into position so that her back rested against his chest. Her hand reached for his arm and draped it across her waist. But when she tried to move his hand onto her breast, he resisted.

"Behave," he said against her ear. "Or I'll leave you alone." He wouldn't really go. With her heat and softness cradled against him, he didn't think anything short of a nuclear disaster could get him to leave. She felt like heaven. Like coming home after a long journey.

"Not good for you to always get your way," Siobahn muttered groggily. Good. The pain pills were starting to work on her.

"I think I could say the same of you...Siobahn."

"Mmm. Like that. Say it again."

"Sleep, Siobahn. I've got you."

CHAPTER SIX

Siobahn was alone in bed when she finally woke. She told herself she wasn't disappointed that Ryker was gone, but she lied. Despite knowing he had a job that required his attention twenty-four-seven, she still felt abandoned.

"Get a grip, girl," she muttered, even as she turned her face into the pillow he'd used and inhaled the lingering traces of his scent. "You're old enough to handle reality."

Problem was, she didn't feel rational when it came to Ryker. She felt greedy to learn everything about him, starved to spend time with him, and possessive as hell.

Recognizing all the signs of one of her romantic crushes—times a thousand—Siobahn distracted herself by making some tentative movements to check her pain level. The pounding in her head had dulled to a faint throb. Her muscles felt stiff, but nothing hurt badly enough to stop her from getting out of bed. Ryker had woken her at regular intervals during the night, checking her pupil response and giving her more pain pills as necessary.

Gingerly, she scooted to the side of the bed and sat up. The world swam for an instant, then settled down. Okay, that was acceptable. She knew from past experience that if the world stayed oriented correctly and her stomach didn't threaten to expel its contents, then she was good to go.

She pushed to her feet and shuffled into the bathroom, her body protesting every inch of the way. Oh, yeah, the aftermath of physical violence was not something she missed about field-work. She'd often ignored threats in order to pursue the truth, so she'd been attacked more than once before. Luck and the self-defense moves her brothers had drilled into her had helped her survive without receiving any life threatening injuries and without being raped.

Staring into the mirror while she waited for the water in the shower to heat up, she carefully removed the gauze on the side of her head. Ugh. A two- maybe three-inch bruise with a cut running down the center marred her left temple. The hair around the wound had been shaved away, but the rest of her hair was long enough that she should be able to hide the bald area until the missing hair grew back.

Overall, it looked nasty, but a gentle probing showed it to be less extensive than it appeared.

This is ridiculous. I cover domestic news now, for pity's sake. Not wars overseas. I'm not supposed to come under this kind of attack again. Still, despite the momentary fear and the lingering pain, she had to admit to feeling alive in a way she hadn't for quite some time.

The hot water from the shower went a long way toward easing the stiffness in her muscles, even as it stung her wound. Still, that didn't stop her from imagining Ryker's strong hands exploring her body.

Having him hold her last night had given her a sense of peace she hadn't realized she was lacking. She usually got home from work late, grabbed a bite to eat and fell exhausted into bed. She'd thought herself content with her life. But sharing body heat with another human being, knowing that there was someone to help her if trouble returned, had soothed her on a very fundamental level.

I must really be getting old if the main reason I want a man in my life is to stop me from feeling so lost and alone.

Lost? Where the hell had that thought come from? Alone, she'd concede. It had been a long time since she'd taken a lover and while she was on good terms with her family and had a close circle of friends, with all the changes at the paper lately she'd rarely had time for visits.

But to call herself lost? Scowling at the uncharacteristic thought, she dried off with a vigor that threatened to revive the monster of all headaches if she didn't ease off.

She wouldn't admit to being lost. Yes, running an investigative team here in D.C. didn't present the same challenge as traveling around the world to crisis points, risking her life in order to be the first, or the only, person to report the truth of a situation. Did her life really lack meaning because she wasn't constantly in danger? Had she become that addicted to adrenaline?

Or was she simply burned out? Fed up with the constant corruption and violence in the world and cynical about the chances of her paper or any other voice making a difference?

No. She had to believe that journalism had a positive role in the world. Otherwise...

She gave a rueful smile. Otherwise her life had been a waste, hadn't it?

Probably it was just the post-adrenaline slump that made her moody and introspective.

But when her left shoulder seized up as she attempted to put her arm into the sleeve of a brushed cotton, button-up shirt, she had to admit that she wasn't the physically resilient woman of twenty years ago. Her shoulder had been badly dislocated during a clash with riot police in Somalia eight years ago and every so often something happened to remind her that her shoulder had never returned to full strength. The damn fall yesterday must have thrown the joint out of whack.

Face it, Siobahn. You're growing old. Fifty is only a few years away.

That's not exactly a death knell. But the butterflies in her belly told a different story. Her high level of natural energy had always seen her through even the roughest patch. The idea that she might be slowing down terrified her.

While her mind still hungered for the challenge of ferreting out the truth, in all honesty, her body didn't take abuse as well as it once did. Cross-training that included aerobics, yoga, running, biking and weight lifting helped keep her in shape. Continued martial arts classes kept her able to react quickly to threat. But last night she hadn't been able to move quickly enough to avoid being tased. That didn't bother her so much as the fact that she hadn't run the instant she opened the door to silence instead of the beep of the alarm.

Trouble was, she'd been too tired and too distracted. The delay in her reaction time had cost her precious seconds she might have used to get away.

On the positive side, she thought as she applied a bit of makeup, last night's attack had brought her closer to Ryker. Not that being a victim was the way she wanted him to think of her, but from the way his body had reacted to holding hers during the night, she was satisfied that the powerful attraction between them was mutual.

He didn't know it yet, but Ryker was going to be hers. Soon, if she could help it. After all, last night proved that danger could strike at any time. And she'd always been one to *carpe diem*.

Smiling to herself, she headed downstairs. The enticing scent of coffee wafted out from her kitchen and her steps quickened in anticipation. Maybe Ryker hadn't left. Maybe—

A dark haired man with the bulk of a linebacker stood at

her stove. Siobahn's heart kicked once in panic, before the man turned around and she recognized Faith's brother. Then she noticed the woman sitting at the far end of the kitchen table.

"Faith! What are you doing here?" Siobahn rushed over to give her friend a hug.

Faith's arms squeezed her before she stepped back, brushing a wayward piece of curly blonde hair out of her face. "Toby heard what happened and volunteered to be one of your guards."

"Er—" Siobahn threw Toby a startled glance. "Hello, Toby. Good to see you."

Both Faith and Toby laughed. "Don't worry, Siobahn," Faith said. "He's stable. Dr. Montague is a genius. Toby has almost no lingering side effects. Ryker has even offered him a job at the SSU. They're just waiting for the separation paperwork to be completed by the DOD."

"Congratulations." Siobahn accepted Toby's gentle hug. "I'm so glad you're okay."

"Thanks, Siobahn." Toby stepped back. "You can call Ryker and verify that I'm cleared for duty, if that would make you more comfortable. And just so you know, there are two SSU men stationed outside, guarding the front and back of the house."

"No. That's fine. I trust Faith. She says you're good to go, so we're cool." No one had fully explained to her what happened to the men in Kerberos's program, just that their minds and bodies had been altered and one of the side effects was uncontrollable rage. Yet she believed Toby wouldn't have been so careful when he hugged her if he'd still been under the full influence of the program.

She looked him over. Aside from having a bit more muscle, and appearing more grim than she remembered, she wouldn't have been able to tell he'd recently been through an ordeal.

"Thanks for helping Faith investigate my disappearance," Toby said.

"My pleasure. I just wish I could have done more."

"You did enough. More than most people who suspected what was going on but kept silent." Toby turned back to the stove, but not before she saw the flash of hurt and anger in his eyes. In his role as a military intelligence officer, he'd been looking into the disappearances of military and law enforcement personnel even before Siobahn. How many people had he worked with that he later learned had been complicit with Kerberos's forced recruitment policies? Had someone Toby trusted been the one to suggest that he be forced into the program?

Her heart ached for him, but she knew he wouldn't want her sympathy.

"Are you hungry?" he asked. "I'm making omelets."

Siobahn raised her brows. "Smart, good looking and you can cook? Tell me again why Faith hasn't married you off?"

Toby laughed and shot an affectionate look at his sister. "We've both been too focused on our careers. Besides, a big brother's first priority has to be watching out for his risk-taking younger sister, not a girlfriend."

"Ah. The old 'I'm married to my job' excuse."

"It's not an excuse if it's true."

Didn't Siobahn know it. Her mood plummeted and she used more force than necessary to pull open the door to the cabinet where she kept the coffee mugs. Between running the investigative team, researching her own stories, and cultivating contacts through networking and socializing, she had next to no free time. Worse, Ryker ran a private special ops group. He'd never be off duty. Was she only fooling herself that she could start something with him? When would either one of them have time? Particularly after he returned to his headquarters in Oregon.

If it's important, you'll make time.

But she was a reporter. The antithesis to the secrecy required within the national security community. What made her think that Ryker would be willing to move forward on his attraction given the threat her job posed?

Siobahn yelped as hot coffee slopped onto her hand. She'd been so immersed in thought, she hadn't noticed the mug over-flowing.

"Careful there," Toby said.

"Yikes." She grabbed a towel and started mopping up the spilled coffee from the counter and floor. "Lost in thought."

"Siobahn." The patient way Faith said her name indicated that she realized something was bothering Siobahn but wasn't going to press for details in front of Toby. "Did Ryker talk to you about moving onto the SSU's Oregon campus until the threat to you has been neutralized?"

Siobahn carefully poured out the excess coffee in her mug, added sugar and cream, and carried it over to the table. "No."

"Well, Toby and I discussed it. We think that you'd be safer out of D.C. The Oregon compound has excellent security and no one would think to look for you there."

But Ryker is in D.C.!

Unwilling to reveal such a weakness, Siobahn just shook her head. "Faith, the paper is in a tight spot right now. Several reporters are either on vacation or on assignment overseas. We're so short staffed that *I've* had to pick up the Capitol beat."

"Poor baby." Faith chuckled.

"Thanks for the sympathy." Siobahn threw a cloth napkin at Faith's head. "You know how much I hate listening to blowhard politicians."

"Yeah, but no one ever said being a reporter was easy. Dangerous, yes. Easy, no. You really should go to Oregon, Siobahn."

She shook her head. "I can't just disappear and abandon my team, making them pick up all the stories I'm working on."

Faith stared at her for a long while. Finally, she sighed. "I expected you to say that." She gave a little self-deprecating laugh. "Neither one of us is good at doing the smart thing, are we?"

Siobahn smiled. "Smart is in the eyes of the beholder." It was a phrase she and Faith had often tossed back and forth when facing critics who thought they should play it safe.

"Safe never won a Pulitzer," Faith agreed.

Siobahn met Faith's eyes and they both burst out laughing.

"What's so funny?" Toby asked.

"The idea that we risked our lives in order to win some damn prize," Faith gasped.

"The truth, the truth, and only the truth shall be my mistress," Siobahn replied with a grin.

Toby glanced back and forth between the two women. "Crazy ladies. Didn't your investigative team win the Pulitzer a few years ago for that series of articles you wrote about child soldiers?"

Siobahn shrugged. "Yeah, but that wasn't our goal during the investigation."

"Simply the icing on the cake," Faith said.

Toby shook his head. "Here, eat." He placed plates of steaming omelets and toast on the table. "Now then, let's plan out your week so you're as safe as possible."

THE ASSASSIN HAD FAILED to take care of the reporter. Myron Zybriesky checked his phone again, confirming that the man he'd had following the reporter had failed to check in. Sighing, he tapped the phone against his chin. Things were not proceeding according to plan.

He paced back and forth in his office. Soon his mysterious

contact would call, expecting to hear that Siobahn Murphy had been eliminated. Yet Myron didn't have any idea what had happened. He'd searched the police blotters and found no mention of an intruder at Murphy's address. Which meant nothing. The DOD, the FBI, even other elements in the CIA might have stepped in and removed the assassin. Or that interfering SSU might have helped the woman.

As an analyst, he didn't have the authority, or the contacts, to order a team to investigate the disappearance of the assassin. But he had a feeling that his contact wouldn't accept such an excuse.

Which meant that it was going to be up to him to eliminate Siobahn Murphy so that no one else would be exposed in this affair.

The question was, how?

"YOU WERE RIGHT, sir. The South Dakota compound appears to be a scaled back version of Kaufmann's lab." Rafe's voice sounded far away. The location his team was investigating was so deep in the wilderness that even the satellite phone connection was poor.

As Ryker listened to the end of Rafe's report, he parked his car a few houses down from Siobahn's place. When he'd realized his destination this evening, he'd questioned his motives. His logical self pointed out that with Toby inside, and Ethan Davies and Tyler Lynch guarding the front and back of the house respectively, Siobahn was well protected. That by showing up unexpected, he was bringing potential trouble to her front door if anyone recognized him. The enemies of the SSU would like nothing better than to find a point of vulnerability to use against Ryker.

Siobahn Murphy was rapidly becoming such a weakness.

Yet this time Ryker's ironclad will was no match for his

instincts. He needed to see Siobahn again. And he needed to warn her that the situation, which they'd thought had been contained, had slipped their control.

"How many enhanced men do you estimate are on site?" he asked Rafe.

"We've counted three teams of twelve. Without getting too close for safety I can't say for certain what level they're at. But based on the way they move, I'm estimating that ninety percent of them are Level 1, with the remainder at Level 2."

Ryker swore. "That means they were brought into the program just before the raid on Kaufmann's compound."

"Yes. So the South Dakota facility must have the ability to administer the drugs and perform the necessary conditioning." From the impartial tone of Rafe's voice, you'd never know that he'd experienced the agony of the drugs burning through his veins or endured hours of torture meant to break him down physically and mentally. Ryker was damn proud of Rafe for surviving.

And he hated the idea that more men were suffering as they spoke. "How's the security?" he asked.

"Tight as a vi—" Rafe cleared his throat and Ryker chuckled. "I've heard and said worse, Rafe."

"Yes, but...ah... It still feels disrespectful, sir."

That right there was one of the issues that was weighing on him, Ryker realized. He missed the tight knit camaraderie that came from being a member of a group of equals.

Odd that this bothered him now, after nearly forty years of running the SSU. Maybe it had been the recent interaction with his Vietnam buddies, and his questioning of their role in the deaths of MacAdam, Jamieson, and Kaufmann that solidified how alone he felt. Maybe it had been seeing how recent events had brought Rafe, Niko, and Kai closer.

Or maybe you're just getting old and tired.

But as he spotted Siobahn's house up ahead, he felt

anything but tired. In fact, knowing he was about to see her again gave him a boost of adrenaline.

"All right," Ryker said. "Send me your report and the surveillance photos. You're set for another two days of observation?"

"Yes, sir."

"Good. By that time I'll know if we're authorized to move in or if we need to stay neutral and let another party do the takedown."

If Rafe had objections to the prospect of another agency taking control, he kept them under wraps.

Once Ryker finished asking his questions, he ended the call.

A few houses down from Siobahn's place, he stopped.

Are you certain this is the right thing to do?

His mind said no. But his gut told him he needed to see her.

CHAPTER SEVEN

"ALL RIGHT," Toby announced, startling Siobahn out of a light doze. "I think I've got something." She'd asked him to use his access to several secure databases to check on the status of Wayne Jamieson and Dr. Kaufmann, since she hadn't seen any reports of their arrests in the news.

Siobahn stood and stretched. "What do you have?" In truth, she didn't want to hear Toby's results right now. She'd been cooped up too long. They'd spent all day researching. After hours of sitting on the couch, Siobahn's whole body felt tight and achy.

"You know what, your news can wait," she said. "Unless you've found information that requires immediate action?"

He shook his head.

"Right. Then I'm out of here." She headed toward the back door, relieved when her stiff hobble eased into a slightly halting limp as her muscles loosened up. "I need to walk."

Toby appeared in front of her, blocking her way with a speed that stole her breath. "Not so fast, lady. You're not going anywhere without protection. Let me call Ethan and inform him that you're heading outside. He can accompany you."

Siobahn grimaced. She hated the necessity of having a guard. "Why don't you and Faith come with me, instead?"

"No. I—"

The front doorbell rang.

Toby grabbed Siobahn's arm and shoved her toward the closet. "Wait inside until—" His cell phone buzzed. After a quick glance down, he relaxed. "Oh. It's Ryker."

Siobahn's body lit up with joy. *Oh, brother. I am in serious trouble.* "Good," she said, quickly sliding into a pair of slip-on sneakers. "He can take me for a walk."

"Er..." The horrified expression on Toby's face made her burst into laughter.

"Relax, Toby, I won't force Ryker to accompany me if he doesn't want to." But feminine instinct told her he wouldn't object.

"Yeah, but, ah...I'm hoping he's going to be my new boss. It would be bad enough guarding just you. But—"

Still chuckling, Siobahn headed for the front door as the bell sounded again. "Hold your horses," she called. "I'm coming."

The fact that she wished she were saying those words under different circumstances had her smile widening as she unlocked and opened the door.

Ryker froze in the middle of texting and stared at her. The relief in his eyes as he spotted her calmed something deep inside Siobahn. The male appreciation as he took in her clingy tunic and tight leggings had her preening. She cocked her hip and leaned against the doorframe. "Hello Ryker with no first name. What a pleasant surprise. What brings you here?"

Not that she had to ask. The way his eyes devoured her was all the answer she needed.

"Good evening, sir. Everything has been quiet here." Toby's crisp report broke the sensual spell.

"Yep," Siobahn agreed. "We're fine here, sir. Perfectly fine.

Doing so well that I was just getting ready to go for a walk." She stepped out the door and looped her arm through Ryker's. Without her heels on, she was a good half foot shorter than him. "You're just in time to escort me."

"Sir, I—" Toby glanced from Siobahn and Ryker to Faith.

Amusement danced in Ryker's eyes. "Stay and protect your sister, Toby. I'm not completely helpless. Ms. Murphy is safe enough with me."

Toby cleared his throat. "With all due respect sir, I know you're still in fighting shape, but we're talking possible attack by enhanced men. I...ah...have something of an advantage in that case. Since both you and Ms. Murphy are under direct threat, I should accompany you. Ethan can watch over Faith."

"Negative. You stay with Faith. Tonelli made a lot of enemies within Kerberos and the CIA when he turned Jamieson over to us. That means Faith is as much a target for being Tonelli's lover as she is for her investigation."

Siobahn chuckled again at the discomfort on Toby's face. Yeah, it didn't matter how old a woman was, big brothers never wanted to hear about their little sister's love life.

She wondered what her brothers would say about her interest in Ryker, who was nearly fifteen years her senior. Would they warn her about getting involved with an older man, one who held such a position of responsibility?

Or would they warn Ryker that Siobahn was a short-term relationship kind of gal and not to let himself get too close to her?

Squelching those thoughts, Siobahn pulled on Ryker's arm. "Come on. I've been cooped up in the house all day. My muscles have positively atrophied from the lack of action. I need to walk to loosen up."

She heard the front door close as Ryker followed her down the stairs. "This way," she said, tugging him to the right.

"There's a walking path that leads along a stream that empties out into the Potomac."

"Sir?" The quiet voice coming out of the bushes to the side of her front steps caused Siobahn to startle and tighten her grip on Ryker's arm.

"It's okay," Ryker said, putting his hand over her fingers. "It's only Ethan."

"Right. I guess I'm still a little jumpy." Something she hated to admit, but somehow the words had just popped out of her mouth.

"Understandable." Ryker turned as a figure stepped out from the bushes. "All right, Ethan, you can follow us. But stay far enough back to give us some privacy."

"Are you armed, sir?"

Siobahn felt Ryker's sigh. His hand moved to his lower back. "Yes."

"Very good, sir."

Siobahn stifled a giggle as she and Ryker walked down the sidewalk. "I feel like a Victorian lady being chaperoned on her date."

Ryker shot her a sideways glance. "Is that what this is? A date?"

She shrugged and gave him a coy smile. "Well, we were supposed to have dinner tomorrow night, weren't we?"

He nodded. "Yes." Some emotion she couldn't define flitted across his face. "Under the circumstances, I think we'd better postpone dinner until the danger has passed."

Siobahn swallowed her disappointment. Ryker might have backed off from their date, but he was with her now and she planned to enjoy his presence. "You never did answer as to why you came to see me tonight. Is something wrong?"

His hesitation lasted so long, she looked up at him. To her surprise, he looked bemused.

"No," he finally answered. "There's nothing wrong." He

cleared his throat and she realized that Ryker was uncomfortable with this discussion. "I just wanted to see you again."

Her heart soared, but her mind insisted on clarification. "And that's bad?"

"I'm quite a bit older than you, Ms.—"

She pinched him and he chuckled. "Vicious woman. All right. I'm quite a bit older than you, Siobahn."

"In case you haven't noticed, that doesn't matter to me. I find you both sexy and fascinating."

His step faltered.

"Oh, my God, have I rattled the great and mighty Director of the SSU?" The idea delighted her. "The man who can face down irate congressmen and navigate the dangers of terrorist threats is thrown off his stride by a little frank talk from a woman?"

"I think you'll find that I'm a bit old-fashioned and conservative when it comes to women," Ryker admitted.

Siobahn's spirits plummeted.

He stroked her hand where it rested on his forearm. "Until now, I've never been attracted to a woman as vibrant and frank as you."

"Is that a problem?"

"Only in that it forces me to adjust my pattern of thinking. We old guys don't take to change very well."

Siobahn pulled him to a stop. "Don't."

At his questioning look, she clarified, "Don't try to set your age up as a barrier between us. I told you, it doesn't matter to me. And I'm pretty damn sure that you possess enough self-confidence to not let it bother you. So if you have a real issue with becoming romantically involved with me, just say it. Otherwise, no more age barbs."

Ryker's silver gray eyes held hers for a very long time. Unable to break away, Siobahn found herself holding her breath. Finally, he sighed and looked away before taking her arm again and continuing down the path along the river. "You're right. I'm sorry. You've caught me at a difficult point in my life. A lot has happened to make me question the choices I've made and the beliefs I've always held to be true. It has me cautious about taking a chance on something new."

She squeezed his arm and pressed companionably against his side. "I understand. You go along thinking that the good guys are always the good guys and then suddenly you discover that they're not and you no longer know who to trust."

"Feeling cynical, Siobahn?"

"Maybe. For years, I kept going on the belief that justice would prevail. As long as I exposed the truth, someone would benefit." She shrugged. "The depth of this whole Kerberos situation has me questioning the institutions I've always trusted." Particularly since MacAdam's death. But she wasn't about to tell Ryker of her suspicions. Not yet. She knew a man with his reputation for integrity wouldn't have sanctioned killing the President, but that didn't mean he'd want Siobahn risking her neck by investigating. For now, what Ryker didn't know wouldn't hurt him and wouldn't cause conflict between them.

She shot him a glance. "Has running the SSU changed your attitude?"

The corner of Ryker's mouth lifted. "Too many years in special ops had already made me cynical before I started the SSU. Let's just say that doing the political tap dance necessary to keep the SSU alive hasn't improved on that."

A calico cat slipped across the path in front of them and disappeared into the bushes. "Don't you ever get tired?" she asked. "Think about chucking it all and doing something completely different?"

Another stroke of his fingers over the back of her hand. It was meant as comfort, but this time her body reacted in a wholly feminine way.

"Have you been thinking of giving up the journalism business Siobahn?"

God, she loved the sound of his voice saying her name. Wait. What had his question been? Oh, that's right. "Maybe. I don't know. I thought I was content. But this week…" She shook her head, which triggered a pulse of headache. "It's been rough. I just don't know if I have the heart to keep going." And why on earth was she saying this to Ryker when the thoughts were so new and unsettling to her?

"Have you considered doing other work?"

She gave a harsh laugh. "No. All I've ever wanted was to be an investigative journalist. I don't even have any hobbies that could turn into a second career." Argh. Could she possibly sound more pathetic?

They passed from a well-lit section of the path into an area where the overhead light had burned out, throwing their section into deeper shadow. "This is a depressing conversation," Siobahn announced.

"What does a girl have to do to get you to kiss her?"

Ryker glanced around and then made a hand gesture back toward the way they'd come. Ethan. That's right. She'd forgotten they had a bodyguard following them.

"Does that mean you're going to kiss me or should I kiss you fir—"

Ryker cut her off by taking her mouth in a kiss that was far more aggressive and dominating than she'd expected from the man who'd been handling her with kid gloves up to now. And oh, Lord, how the man could kiss. She would've sworn that her memory of their previous kiss had been faulty. That the tender way he'd kissed her before hadn't caused such a powerful reaction in her.

She'd have been wrong.

The world simply melted away under the sensual assault of his mouth. He didn't allow her time to get used to the fierce, demanding pressure of his lips before he softened the kiss. She sighed, accepting the languid movement of his tongue in her mouth. Absorbing the tantalizing taste of him.

They explored one another gently at first, then playfully, with teasing nips and quick forays with their tongues that had her squirming to get closer in a vain attempt to ease the ache between her legs.

One of his hands cradled the back of her head and the other settled at the small of her back, urging her hips into firmer contact with him. She whimpered and clutched his back, trying to eliminate the distance between them as the kiss once again turned aggressive.

Siobahn finally pulled back for breath, already mourning the heat of his mouth. But he didn't release her. Instead, his mouth slid along her jaw, down her neck and settled over the pulse point at the base of her throat. When he suckled the skin into his mouth, her whole body jerked with arousal.

His hand slipped from the small of her back to trace the crease between her buttocks. Suspended by the magic he was creating with his mouth and his hand, Siobahn felt her arousal crank impossibly higher. It was too much. "If you keep this up," she gasped. "I'm going to come right here."

Ryker stilled. He swiped his tongue once more along her skin, then straightened and let his hand fall away.

"Dammit, I didn't want you to stop just..." She blinked up at him through the haze of sexual confusion.

"I know. But we're in public. Ethan might be turned partially away to give us privacy, but he's keeping us in his periphery vision. If I didn't stop then, I might have gone too far." He bent down to whisper the next words in her ear. "I want privacy when I take you."

At her gasp, he smiled down at her, then ran his thumb across her lower lip. "Did that answer your question about the kiss?"

"What? Oh. Yeah." She cleared her throat. "I mean, yes. All I have to do is push you and you'll give me what I want."

Ryker gave a crack of laughter, then placed a quick, hard kiss on her lips. "I like you, Siobahn Murphy. I really do. But don't think I'll always let you get your way." He hooked his arm through hers and turned her back toward the house. "Come on. Let's get you home."

"Will you stay with me again tonight?"

She felt his muscles tense under her fingers. "I don't think that would be a very good idea."

"Why?"

"You're still recovering from your head injury." The look he slanted toward her could only be called wicked. "And after that kiss, I don't trust myself just to hold you."

"Pooh." She stuck out her lower lip. "Really? You're going to make me sleep in my house all alone the night after I was attacked?"

He laughed. "No. I figured Toby and Faith would be willing to stay with you."

"But I want you."

"And I want to stay with you. But I'm not joking, Siobahn. My control isn't what it should be around you. I—"

"Maybe I don't need your control."

"Siobahn, when we get back to your place, take a look in the mirror. You're looking pale and pinched. And your steps have slowed considerably since we turned around. The kiss set your head to pounding again, didn't it?"

"How did you know?" she grumbled. "Maybe I just don't want to go home yet."

Ryker halted. "Would you like to keep walking, Ms. Murphy?"

"No," she admitted with a growl. "Damn you, you're right. And damn you for reminding me that I was recently a victim. I hate that."

"I know. And I'm sorry. But as I said, I tend to be old-fashioned about women. One of my beliefs is that a man should look out for the health of the lady he's with. And since you clearly intended on ignoring your pain until you dropped..."

Siobahn smacked his shoulder, then winced as the sharp movement aggravated her headache. "Word of advice, here. Independent women don't like being forced into positions of weakness or reminded that they have vulnerabilities."

Ryker lowered his voice. "Not even in bed? Come on, Siobahn. Are you telling me you've never let a man dominate you during lovemaking? Never had a man tie you down and then spend hours exploring your body?"

Hours? She swallowed. Damn him. How dare he turn the tables and become blatantly sexual when she was already off balance? Now the idea of being held helpless while Ryker explored her body had her clit throbbing. "That," she said stiffly, "is something you're going to have to wait to find out for yourself."

Ryker's teeth nipped the top of her ear lobe. "I look forward to it."

He straightened up. A few steps later, he nodded to the shadows and Siobahn realized that they'd reached Ethan's position. Great. Just how much had he seen? Or heard?

When they'd passed the man by, Siobahn whispered to Ryker, "Will the fact that Ethan saw you kissing me undermine your authority?"

Ryker turned his head toward her in surprise. "What? No. If anything, it will only add to the respect. Not only do I kick ass on the dojo floor, but I can win the attention of a beautiful woman like yourself. And trust me, none of my men would ever think less of you for being caught in a kiss with me. They'll be curious to see what type of woman has so enchanted me that I forgot propriety and kissed you in public, but they won't treat you with any less respect because of it. The SSU doesn't tolerate sexual harassment. Men who think that women are easy and therefore suitable prey don't get invited to join the SSU. Contrary to the recent media reports of sexual assault in the military, most soldiers honor and protect women. They don't hurt or intimidate them."

"Wow. Sorry. Didn't mean to hit one of your trigger issues."

"No. It's my fault. I apologize. Your brothers and father are military and law enforcement men. You don't need me preaching at you."

"That's all right." They walked several feet in silence. "Do you want to talk about it?"

Ryker took a deep breath. His mouth pressed into a thin line before he answered. "I developed some very strong friendships during my service in Vietnam. Most of which have lasted to today. The man I was closest to, Eric Paterson, joined the SSU soon after I founded it, and then brought his son Kai into the organization after Kai decided to leave the CIA. I won't go into the details now, but due to an undercover assignment I gave Kai, Eric, his wife, and his teenage son and daughter—twins—were brutally murdered. And...scalped."

"Oh, my God. Ryker." Siobahn squeezed his arm. "I'm so sorry."

"Eric's wife and youngest daughter were raped before they died. Jenna, his oldest daughter, was also raped and partially scalped. She survived. Barely."

Siobahn heard the anguish in his voice, strong even after all this time. Her heart ached with the need to soothe his pain away.

"Kai had called to warn me that his cover had been blown and his family was in imminent danger. But I didn't receive the message in time. Someone had deleted his voicemail from my phone. It was sheer luck that I needed to retrieve another message, went into the deleted messages archive, and heard his warning. I immediately called to warn Eric. He planned to evacuate the family and meet me at the airport. When no one showed, I headed to the house."

He swallowed loud enough for Siobahn to hear. "Paramedics were carrying out body bags when I arrived. My warning had come too late."

Siobahn rested her head on Ryker's shoulder in a silent show of support, knowing he wouldn't want to hear her say it wasn't his fault.

"I'd promised Eric that I would take care of his family if anything happened to him, but I failed him. The best I could do was bring Jenna to the medical center at the SSU and make sure that while she recovered she would be hidden from the man who'd targeted her family, Mexican crime lord Jaime Alvarez."

"I remember Alvarez," she said. "There was a big stink when he got out of prison. Accusations that he'd bribed or intimidated a judge into reducing his sentence." She searched her memory. "Then Alvarez died in a shootout in Mexico. Right?"

"Yes."

Siobahn suspected there was more to Alvarez's death than had been reported, but wasn't going to ask for details.

"How's Jenna now?"

"She eventually made a full recovery."

Again, something in Ryker's tone made Siobahn think there was more to the story. Yet all she said was, "You're proud of her."

"Yes. She's like a daughter to me." He smiled. "Jenna recently married one of my more experienced agents, a man named Niko Andros. She's now helping with a couple of rehabilitation programs we run for our wounded agents. And her brother Kai is part of the medical team that helped bring Toby back to normal."

"Small world."

"Special ops often is. It gets narrower, though." Ryker took a deep breath and some of the tension that had eased from his shoulders crept back in. "Rafe Andros, Niko's brother, was captured by Dr. Kaufmann and put through the enhanced soldier program. A doctor who defected from Kaufmann's lab, Dr. Gabrielle Montague, led the team that brought Rafe back to sanity. Her work is key to helping all of Kaufmann's victims."

"You feel responsible. Both for what happened to the Patersons, and for Rafe's capture."

"Of course. They were mine to protect and I failed them."

Unable to hold her emotions in any more, she stepped in front of Ryker and looked up at him. "That's what makes you such an admirable leader. You care for your people. You take responsibility for their well being, even when there was nothing you could have done to prevent the tragedies." She brushed her lips against his.

"Thank you for sharing this with me," she murmured.

A wry smile touched his mouth. "What is it about you, lady, that lowers all my defenses and has me spilling my guts?" He leaned down and gave her a kiss that was more about two human beings being grateful to have found one another than it was about arousal.

Then he tucked her back against his side and put his arm around her waist.

They walked back to her place in silence.

CHAPTER EIGHT

Ryker didn't know how Siobahn did it. Last night she'd somehow managed to convince him to once again hold her while she slept. Whereas the previous night Siobahn's injured status had cooled his body's reaction, last night, with the taste of her still lingering in his mouth, Ryker had found it excruciatingly difficult to stop himself from rolling over, trapping her soft, willing body beneath him, and thrusting inside her.

Now, with the warm, soft length of her body draped across his chest, the early morning sunlight picking out dark highlights in her magnificent red hair, he struggled to remember why stroking his hand down her back like this was a bad idea. Siobahn made a sleepy, contented little sound and shifted. The new position put Ryker's hand at the hem of her sleep tee where it rested just below the waistband of her loose shorts. Wondering how far he could go before she woke up, he slipped his fingers underneath the thin cotton until they met the silken skin of her lower back.

Just that relatively innocent touch sent fire through his veins. Needing more, his lips pressed against her temple. As his fingers walked up the bumps of her spine, his tongue darted out to taste her skin.

"Mmm," Siobahn murmured sleepily, arching into his hand. "Feels good."

Ryker spread his fingers out, drawing random patterns on her back as his hand inched toward her shoulders. The t-shirt, caught on his wrist, rose to expose her creamy skin to the golden light.

When his hand reached the back of her neck, the t-shirt stretched, its front trapped between their bodies. Siobahn made a sound of annoyance, lifted her upper body, and yanked off the shirt. Then her fingers delved under Ryker's undershirt and before he knew it they lay skin to skin.

"Much better," Siobahn muttered, settling against his side with one arm nestled between their bodies and the other draped across his chest. Ryker might have thought she'd fallen back asleep, except her fingers drifted across his bare skin, stopping to first circle then pinch his nipples before moving on.

When she shifted over him to take one stiff nipple into her mouth, his hips rose involuntarily. "Siobahn!"

"You taste good," she whispered, moving to tongue the other nipple.

"If you don't stop that, we're going to end up with a fast finish," Ryker warned as his erection strained to be free of his boxers.

The look she shot him was full of feminine mischief. "Is that a problem?"

"It is if you're not completely ready."

In response, she shimmied out of her shorts and panties, then grabbed his hand and put it between her legs. Hot, silken honey slid over his fingers. He groaned.

At the press of her hips, he slipped first one, then two fingers inside her and pressed his thumb against her clit.

"Oh, my, yes." Siobahn closed her thighs, trapping his hand as she moved against him.

"No." He pulled his hand back and turned Siobahn onto her back, holding her in place with one hand on her softly rounded belly as he shucked out of his boxers. "We're not going to rush this." He paused and took a moment to just admire the way she was spread out in front of him on the bed, the red of her hair a bright contrast against the pale green sheets.

She arched her back, thrusting her breasts higher. He loved that she wasn't ashamed of her feminine curves, the occasional age lines and the dimples of cellulite on her body. Her confident smile, proclaiming that she knew he found her attractive, only jacked his arousal higher.

He wanted to spend those hours exploring her body that he'd promised, but one glance at the clock and he realized he didn't have much time before he had to head to the office.

Siobahn noticed the direction of his gaze and frowned.

"Don't worry," he said, settling between her legs. He pressed a kiss to her throat. "I'm not going to leave you unsatisfied."

Her hand reached down and circled him. "I should hope not. That would be incredibly...painful for you."

Her throaty comment had him laughing against her mouth. Then gasping as her fingers squeezed. In retaliation, his hand found and kneaded her breast. When he tweaked her nipple, she gave a little cry and her grip on him loosened. "Hmm. Have I found a weakness in the mighty Siobahn Murphy?"

Her answer was to run her fingernails along his length while her teeth nipped at the juncture between his neck and shoulder. "Enough." He was already so hard he was about to burst. "Condom?"

She nodded toward the bedside table.

Ryker was shocked to see his hand shaking as he opened the foil packet and slipped the condom on. Siobahn also must have noticed, because she took his mouth in a deep kiss.

Breaking the kiss, she smiled that seductress's smile and guided him inside her until he was fully seated within her wet heat.

For a long moment Ryker held still, staring in wonder at the woman looking back at him with desire and something even warmer in her bewitching green eyes. With a small movement of her hips, she encouraged him to move.

Well aware that there was an SSU agent within earshot and that the bedroom door wasn't locked, Ryker pressed a finger to Siobahn's lips to indicate silence as he began to thrust slowly in and out of her. Her wicked smile turned into gasps and soft cries that he muffled with his mouth as his rhythm picked up speed.

He felt her inner muscles clench a second before she tore her mouth from his and arched her neck. She bit her lip as her climax took her, stifling her cry of completion. Ryker thrust one more time deep inside her then buried his face in the pillow to muffle his own shout as his semen jetted out of him.

Siobahn's fingers smoothed down his back as he relaxed against her.

"Well, that was certainly a lovely wakeup call," she whispered against his ear. "Let's do that again. Soon."

Ryker chuckled. "It will be my pleasure." He snuck another glance at the clock. "But now I need to go."

She sighed. "Don't go, Ryker."

"I have to." He paused. "And it's Ryan."

"What?"

Ryker gave her a mischievous smile. "My name. Ryker is short for Ryan Broderick Kerrigan the Third. My teammates in Vietnam shortened Ryan Kerrigan into Ryker. Because my parents and I had a major falling out regarding my war service, I've gone by Ryker ever since. But legally, my name is still Ryan Kerrigan."

"Which is why I couldn't find any information on Ryker when I searched the Internet."

"Yes. That and the fact that the SSU buries information about its employees for security reasons."

She nodded. "Makes sense. Should I call you Ryan, then?"

"Absolutely not. It's Ryker."

"Hmm..."

Laughing, he kissed her again. A few minutes later, he finally detached himself and padded into the bathroom to dispose of the condom. He took a quick shower, dressed in yesterday's clothes, and returned to the bedroom.

Only to find that Siobahn had fallen asleep.

He quietly let himself out of the room, then left the house.

"Good morning, sir."

Ryker nodded to Alain McCormick, a new member of the team who'd come highly recommended from Faith's brother Toby. The slight curl to McCormick's mouth let Ryker know that the news he'd spent a second night at Siobahn's house would be all over the SSU by noon. No one gossiped more than a tight-knit group of soldiers or spies.

Striding down the block toward the place he'd left his car, Ryker wondered what his team would think if they saw the hickey Siobahn had left on him. Grinning to himself, he beeped open his car's doors and slid behind the wheel.

He'd just cranked the engine when his phone chirped. The text message from General Wehrig held him frozen with a combination of fear and hope.

Meeting of gang of five. Same time and place as last time.

Today the pang of grief that came from seeing the number five, instead of six as it had been when Eric Paterson had been alive, was sharper than it had been in a long while. Probably because his talk with Siobahn had awoken memories of the man he'd considered his best friend.

I'll be there, Ryker typed back.

He checked his watch. It was a good thing he had a change of clothes at the office, because he didn't have time to go home first. There was too much data he needed to put together for this meeting.

National Arboretum
Washington, D.C.

RYKER WALKED WARILY toward the picnic table at the National Arboretum. Several months ago this group of former soldiers from Vietnam had met to discuss the possibility that the President of the United States had ordered the murder of thousands of innocent people.

With MacAdam, Kaufmann and Jamieson all dead, Ryker wasn't certain if he could still trust his friends. Only someone who knew about the anniversary demonstration and had top-level security clearance could have arranged for the deaths.

Someone like the men seated around the table. Yet they'd been through hell together, so until he found proof, he'd give them each the benefit of the doubt.

"Gentlemen," he said, nodding politely as he stopped several yards away from the table. His caution prompted one "What the fuck" and a couple of speculative frowns.

"Before I come any closer, I need assurance from each of you that you had nothing to do with the deaths of President MacAdam, Dr. Kaufmann and Wayne Jamieson."

Their expressions ranged from outrage to relief to disappointment. Ryker realized that some of them had held the same doubts about him. Which only made sense. The knowledge of the whole affair had been confined to a select group, making each man here a suspect in the murders.

One by one, Ryker's friends looked him in the eye and gave him the assurance he needed, easing the knot that had formed in his gut when he first suspected one of them had betrayed everything he believed they stood for.

"I swear to you by the honor of spec ops team Achilles One that I did not order, have prior knowledge of, or condone the murder of President MacAdam, Dr. Kaufmann or Wayne Jamieson." Brit Remington, head of the House Judiciary Committee, swore his oath with a grim smile, then turned to General Aldrick Wehrig.

Wehrig, dressed today in casual civilian clothes like the others, sighed, then lifted his eyes from his perusal of the battered canvas messenger bag sitting in front of him. "I had no idea there was any threat of murder ahead of time, but the autopsies made me suspicious. The faint traces of a top-secret chemical indicated involvement by someone in our neurotoxin research branch." He opened the bag and pulled out four manila envelopes, which he distributed among the group.

Ryker, hearing the true regret in his friend's voice, took his envelope and sat down.

"Captain Armand Devraiz," Wehrig said, "was the leader of a team of researchers in our biochemical weapons department. He joined shortly after Nevsky's death and pushed hard to continue Nevsky's research into creating a super soldier. When it became clear that the funding did not exist for a program that had such deadly side effects, he went silent on the topic. Switched his focus to creating antidotes to weaponized neurotoxic substances."

Ryker sat very still, dreading where this would lead.

"Nine days ago, one of Devraiz's assistants died in the lab after inhaling fumes released from a broken beaker. The body disappeared before it could be autopsied. One of the other assistants in the lab later reported that she'd overheard a conversation indicating that Devraiz had been responsible for removing the body. When we moved in to question Devraiz, he panicked. He took the lab assistant hostage, then threatened to disperse a toxin into the building's air ducts if we didn't let him leave."

"What happened?" Matt Jordaine of the FBI asked.

"He'd forgotten that everyone at the DOD gets weapons and self-defense training. The assistant fought back and broke free. Devraiz was shot in the ensuing struggle. On the way to the hospital, the ambulance was ambushed and Devraiz escaped." Wehrig glanced down at the briefcase. "Unfortunately, in the aftermath, our inventory turned up several missing toxins. We've started a manhunt for Devraiz and have to assume that he has the ability to release those toxins on the public or any pursuers."

"Christ," Jordaine said. "Why weren't any of us notified? This guy has been running around for nine damn days?"

Wehrig sat up straighter. "I only just found out about it myself. It seems that certain elements within the DOD ordered an information blackout after they discovered encrypted files on Devraiz's home computer that suggested he provided the neurotoxin that was used to kill President MacAdam and the others. Unfortunately, our investigators still haven't discovered whether Devraiz acted alone or was taking orders from someone else."

Ryker cursed. The expressions of the other men around the table mirrored the anger he felt.

"On another note," Wehrig continued, "we've uncovered what we believe to be the last of the DOD employees who helped Jamieson target and kidnap soldiers who met Kaufmann's requirements."

"That brings me to my news," Ryker said. "I've just received confirmation from an SSU reconnaissance team that a newly discovered compound in South Dakota has at least three teams of men that show signs of being enhanced by a program similar to Kaufmann's." Ryker placed several photographs on the table.

"Dammit, I thought we'd found all the victims," Remington snapped. "Just how many offshoots did Kaufmann have?"

"It gets worse," Roger Brown commented. "The CIA has

implemented extra security measures in the aftermath of Jamieson's deception. We've placed hidden cameras and microphones in the areas surrounding Jamieson's office and the suite of offices he used for Kerberos's headquarters." He added another photograph to the pile in the middle of the table. "This is Myron Zybriesky, a former analyst for Kerberos who was shifted into another department. He's talking with a man we've identified as former Lance Corporal Gene Franzia."

The former Marine wore one of Kaufmann's distinctive black uniforms. Ryker recognized the man as Siobahn's intruder and again noticed the unfamiliar multicolored stripe on his collar.

Brown nodded at the photo. "We have tape showing Franzia looking lost and confused when he discovered that Jamieson and Kerberos's offices were empty. Zybriesky informed him that Jamieson was dead and that Kerberos no longer existed. Franzia admitted to being one of Kerberos's newest assassins and that he needed new directions."

"Data suggests that Kaufmann had also continued the second branch of Nevsky's research," Ryker interjected. "One focused on creating mind-controlled, superintelligent spies and assassins." He tapped the picture of Franzia. "I believe the multicolored stripe indicates Franzia was part of this second branch of the program."

"The mind control would explain why Franzia agreed so eagerly to follow Zybriesky's orders," Brown said. "Which were—"

"To follow and then kill newspaper editor and reporter Siobahn Murphy," Ryker finished for him.

"Yes. I gather the SSU intervened?"

"Correct." Ryker explained what had happened. "We sent Franzia to our laboratory facility in Georgia. Initial blood tests suggest he was given chemical compounds similar to those found in the other victims from Kaufmann's lab, but in Franzia's blood these compounds were combined with other, as yet unidentified substances. The man appears to have faster reflexes and above average strength, but not to possess the extreme bulk that we have seen with the other victims."

Ryker gave each one of his friends a glance. "We've asked for the man's consent to reverse the effects, primarily the mind control, but he's refused. Since cognitive tests show he retains enough self-awareness to make such a decision, we're not going to proceed against his wishes." Remington nodded approval.

"At this point," Ryker continued, "the only legal reason to hold him is for breaking into Ms. Murphy's home and using a Taser on her that resulted in a fall and a concussion."

There were several murmurs of condemnation.

"We'll take him back," Wehrig said. "Technically, since he's not dead, he's AWOL."

"At this time, we don't know whether he'll remain mentally stable," Ryker warned. "Or how he'll react to being cut off from a handler. Our medical team reports that he seems fidgety. Agitated. I believe it would be wiser to keep him with the SSU until we better understand his situation. The medical team needs to determine whether his body is deteriorating in the same way as Kaufmann's physically enhanced soldiers."

"Understood."

"Has there been any progress in locating backup files for either Kaufmann or Jamieson?" Remington asked.

Ryker shook his head at the same time Jordaine said, "No."

"It's possible that the South Dakota facility is also serving as a backup center," Ryker said. "We'll know for certain once we get inside."

He glanced at Jordaine. "I'm assuming you want the SSU to head this."

Jordaine nodded. "Yes. We still haven't located whoever was responsible for picking the FBI and Homeland Security agents to be conscripted into Kaufmann's program."

"All right. Rafe Andros is team leader on this. He'll know how best to proceed."

Wehrig nodded. "Good to know Andros is back up to speed. It was a terrible thing that happened to him. Just terrible."

The group gave murmurs of agreement.

"In the meantime, if there are men and women you trust implicitly," Ryker said, "I suggest you ask them about any new disappearances in their ranks. Rafe thinks the men in South Dakota aren't more than six weeks into the program, which means they were nabbed after we took down Kaufmann's lab. Making the odds good that the South Dakota compound can carry out the complete program on its own."

More somber nods.

"All right then," Wehrig said. "The DOD will continue to search for Devraiz." He glanced at Jordaine. "With help from the FBI?"

Jordaine nodded. "In conjunction with the DOD and the SSU, the FBI will continue its search for the victims of Kaufmann's program." He shot a glance at Ryker. "Which will now include locating any of Kerberos's enhanced spies and assassins."

"The CIA will keep tabs on Zybriesky," Brown said. "If he's trying to restart Kerberos, he'll need outside help."

"The SSU will continue to investigate the compound in South Dakota and report back. Also, once we determine Franzia is stable enough, we'll turn him over to the DOD."

"I'll continue to work with the current President and deflect any members of Congress who get too close to the truths we're under oath to keep secret." Remington didn't quite manage to keep the distaste off his face, a sentiment Ryker agreed with.

"All of us need to consider who has the power and the clearance to order the murder of the President," Jordaine added. "I trust we're all taking extra security measures to ensure we're not next."

The grumbled agreements had Ryker fighting back a smile. Due to their busy, mainly administrative jobs, most of the men at the table were no longer in fighting shape. Jordaine was the only other man fit enough to offer a challenge if physically attacked. Not that his friends would ever admit out loud to needing protection. Still, Ryker knew they'd take the necessary precautions. They might be proud, but none of them had survived this long by being stupid.

Despite knowing more men were currently suffering under Kaufmann's program, Ryker felt more optimistic than before as he said good-bye to his friends and headed back to the office. Confirming that his friendship with these men hadn't been built on a lie was a staggering relief.

It felt right to be working as a team again. Realizing how much he'd missed them, Ryker vowed that when this was over he'd make more of a point to keep in regular touch with the men who were the closest thing he had to brothers.

CHAPTER NINE

Siobahn shut down her office computer with a sigh. She'd just sent her team's final installment in their latest story to the editorial director.

I'm really sick of these late hours. I honestly don't want to be working here this time next year.

Whoa. Where had that thought come from?

Siobahn thought back to her conversation with Ryker, but knew that her discontent had been building for some time. Even while she'd been trying to coax Faith back into taking her old job as a reporter, part of Siobahn had hoped she could convince her friend to take over running the investigative team. But after spending time with Faith, Siobahn realized that she really wasn't going to return. Whether running her local high school newspaper and teaching journalism would sustain Faith's investigative instincts for long, Siobahn couldn't say. But her friend had that rare glow of true happiness. Not even at the height of Faith's career as an investigative journalist had she looked so satisfied.

Her new lover must be amazing.

That was something else different. Faith claimed that for

security purposes, she couldn't tell Siobahn the name of the man she'd fallen in love with. All she'd say was that he had played an important part in helping rescue Toby. Apparently, until any fallout from that situation had been dealt with, the man needed to remain anonymous.

Denying Siobahn information was the surest way to drive her to distraction, but at the same time, she completely understood the need for privacy. Particularly when it came to romantic relationships. She might have been something of a serial dater back in her day—ugh, that made her sound like some aging grande dame—but she'd never gone around flaunting her conquests. She'd only shared the details of her love life with a select group of friends.

Faith had always been one of those confidants. Yet Siobahn hadn't told her about Ryker. Yes, she was certain her friend knew that Ryker had spent the night twice, but since Faith hadn't brought it up, Siobahn had been unwilling to do so. After all, what was she going to say? I think I'm falling for Toby's new boss? And oh, by the way, the sex was amazing?

She didn't even trust her own judgment. What if these feelings for Ryker were simply a result of stress combined with burnout? Was this her midlife crisis? Did women in their late forties even qualify for the term midlife crisis?

Muttering curses under her breath, she shut off her office light and headed into the nearly empty maze of cubicles. Alain McCormick, the SSU agent who'd been guarding her all day, detached himself from the wall he'd been leaning against. With his military short dark hair, his black t-shirt and cargo pants, and his sleekly muscled physique, his appearance screamed bodyguard. More than one female colleague had stopped by Siobahn's office today, ostensibly to find out what was going on with Siobahn in the aftermath of the FBI's raid. But in truth, Siobahn's colleagues had just wanted to ogle McCormick. The man handled the attention with surprising good humor, flirting back without losing his focus.

If she'd been younger and hadn't already met Ryker, Siobahn would have staked her own claim on her sexy protector. But while she appreciated McCormick's hotness factor, he didn't fire up her libido the way Ryker did.

"Ready to go home?" McCormick asked.

Siobahn shook her head. "I have a meeting with a contact." She gave him a stern look. "The person I'm meeting is skittish, so you're going to need to stay hidden, okay?"

"I'm not going to put your life at risk, Ms. Murphy. Director Ryker would have my hide."

Siobahn blinked. Hmm. What was Ryker like when he lost his temper? She'd bet he got all quiet, chilling the other person out, in stark contrast to the fiery eruption that was the standard Murphy way of displaying temper.

"I'll explain to Ryker that any harm that befalls me is entirely my own fault," Siobahn reassured him.

"Sorry, ma'am, but that's not good enough. If I determine the location is too much of a security threat, I *will* prevent you from entering. Even if I have to knock you out and drag you to safety."

God, he sounded just like one of her brothers. "You take your duty seriously, don't you?"

"Yes, ma'am. Doubly so, since it's obvious the boss has a... um...personal interest in your safety."

Well, didn't that just make her blush. Angry that she felt embarrassed over his knowledge of the growing relationship between herself and Ryker, Siobahn strode down the walkway that separated the two rows of cubicles. A few distracted good-byes and good nights from late-shift reporters followed her out.

"Where are we headed?" McCormick asked.

"The National Museum of Lab Detectives up on Seventh."

"Aren't they closed?"

"Yes, that's the point." With the popularity of interactive museums like the International Spy Museum and the National Museum of Crime and Punishment, the National Museum of Lab Detectives had opened last year, documenting forensic and medical examination techniques used in solving crimes. Because the museum displayed actual forensic samples from some very high profile cases, the security around the building was excellent. "My contact, Dr. Robert Penfield, works part-time at the museum."

What McCormick didn't need to know was that Siobahn had met Robert while dating his younger brother. She'd ended her brief affair with the brother years before, but she and Robert had remained friends.

She also wasn't sure how much McCormick knew about the mystery surrounding the death of MacAdam, so for now she wasn't going to tell him that Robert had been a member of the team analyzing samples from the former president's body. According to the panicked phone call she'd received earlier, he'd been trying to isolate and identify an unknown substance found in the President's blood.

"I'm scared, Siobahn," Robert had admitted. "I think I'm being followed, so I've been living at the museum and using their state-of-the-art facility."

Because Robert had given her a tour right after the museum opened, Siobahn knew that at the end of the final gallery a one-way mirror overlooked a forensic lab, allowing museum patrons to watch the scientists and doctors at work. However, deep in the bowels of the museum where the public wasn't allowed, there was a second, highly sophisticated lab that handled confidential and complicated cases. That would be where Robert had holed up.

"I think I've finally identified a marker that indicates where the unusual substance in MacAdam's blood might have come from," Robert had added. "You're the only one I trust to help me get this information to someone in authority who isn't involved in the cover-up."

So Siobahn had promised to meet him tonight.

Siobahn strode across the brightly lit parking garage, McCormick by her side. With the threat against her unresolved, Ryker had insisted that she was safer driving to work than taking the Metro, as she preferred.

When they reached her car, McCormick held out his hand for the keys.

"No," Siobahn said. "I'll drive."

"Wrong. It's safer for me to drive. I'm trained in defensive driving."

She smirked. "So am I."

If he was surprised, he didn't show it. "Bet my rating is more recent and higher than yours. Give over."

"Damn you." She blew out a breath and dropped the keys into his hand. Because she didn't drive much these days, she hadn't taken a refresher course recently.

McCormick accepted his win without gloating, which she appreciated. Her brothers would have crowed with triumph and continued to rub it in for hours.

The museum was in a part of the city occupied mostly by office buildings, which meant that at this hour the streets were nearly deserted. The lack of activity gave the neighborhood a slightly sinister feel and Siobahn had the fleeting thought that maybe she should have told Ryker about this meeting. But, she really didn't want to scare Robert off. And the museum sounded like a secure enough place to meet.

Ten minutes later, McCormick found a parking space one door down from the museum's front entrance. Holding back her impatience, Siobahn waited while McCormick spent several minutes visually inspecting the street before he declared it safe.

The second he gave the all clear, she jumped out of the car.

"I'm accompanying you, else you're not going in," McCormick warned as he checked out the front of the building.

"I—" Siobahn glanced through the plate glass windows and frowned at the pitch black interior. "That's odd. Robert said that the light over the ticket sales counter was always on." Her hand reached for the door handle but strong masculine fingers closed over hers.

"It's better if you don't leave any fingerprints." Ryker's hot breath against her ear sent her body into overdrive.

"Where the hell did you come from?" she demanded on a shaky breath.

Her only response was an amused burst of air against her temple. "Don't think you're going to get all my secrets, Ms. Murphy." The tip of his tongue briefly touched the rim of her ear and she shivered. "Not yet, anyway."

"Sir!"

As Ryker stepped away, Siobahn shot a glare at McCormick and narrowed her eyes as Ethan Davies moved into position on McCormick's left. Ethan must have accompanied Ryker.

"When did you have time to call them?" she demanded of McCormick.

"I listened in on your conversation this afternoon and passed the information on."

"Why, you sneak!"

McCormick shrugged unrepentantly. "Just doing my job."

"You should have contacted me yourself," Ryker chided. "I thought you knew better than to put yourself in danger."

"I—" Siobahn scowled. "It's—Oh, forget it." She crossed her arms over her chest. "Someone should have been protecting Robert and the others who were analyzing—" She cut her eyes over to McCormick and Ethan and shut up, in case they weren't supposed to know that MacAdam's samples had been sent to multiple labs. In fact, she didn't even know if Ryker was aware of that fact.

Ryker gave her a nod. "You're right. That aspect of security was being handled by a different group. Since we've seen no signs of other security personnel, that makes this situation even more dangerous." He tugged her away from the door. "McCormick, we'll follow you inside."

"Right, sir." The man removed a pair of thin leather gloves from his jacket, pulled out a compact flashlight and tried the door. "It's unlocked, sir."

Ryker tensed beside her. "Ethan, call in a break-in. You might not be able to get police support, given tonight's concert on the Mall. So tell Alpha Team to mobilize and head over here. Then guard the entrance. Siobahn, I want you—"

She pushed past him. "Ro—" Before she could finish calling her friend's name, Ryker put his hand over her mouth.

"Don't announce that we're here," he said softly, "in case Dr. Penfield isn't alone, or this is a trap."

"Oh," she said against his fingers. Then, in retaliation for his earlier tease, she licked him.

Her reward was a sharp inhale. "Vixen," he murmured against her cheek with enough sensual promise to make her squirm.

McCormick cleared his throat, but his voice still sounded faintly strangled when he spoke. Whether he was biting back shock or amusement, Siobahn didn't want to know. "Ah...which way Ms. Murphy?"

Cheeks heating, Siobahn pulled away from Ryker. In an attempt to regain some control of the situation, she reached into her purse for her mini-flashlight. Shining the light around the lobby, she tried to orient herself. "The whole place must have lost power," she whispered. Not even a glimmer of light shone from the corners of the room. "But shouldn't the emergency exit signs still be lit? Wouldn't they have a separate power source?"

"Yes. Those would have to be disabled separately." Ryker's

flashlight beam combined with the other two to provide a sufficient amount of light for navigation.

Siobahn walked slowly over to the ticket counter. Robert
had met her in the lobby before taking her through the public
part of the museum, which started upstairs on the right. So
which way was the lab from here?

Memory slowly returned. "If we go through the gift shop,
there's a staircase to the lower level. I think there's a back
door on the second landing that leads to the private labs."
She'd been surprised to learn that actual forensic work took
place behind the scenes. Work that the public never saw.
Robert had explained that taking cases for overworked law
enforcement departments provided much needed cash while
the museum built its reputation as a must-see tourist
destination.

"Which way?" McCormick asked.

"Left."

"Siobahn, stay next to me," Ryker said.

"Okay." Since she didn't particularly want to end up
grabbed by a bad guy in the dark, she had no problem agreeing. And she would totally ignore the fact that being ordered
around by Ryker turned her on.

As they navigated between the gift shop display cases and
racks holding museum themed t-shirts, Siobahn didn't mind
admitting that she felt safer walking between Ryker and
McCormick. There was just something primitively scary about
walking through the dark, silent room.

"There," she said quietly, pointing to the doorway to their
right. A metal gate about seven feet tall stopped visitors who
hadn't paid the entrance fee from taking the back way into the
museum's galleries. Ryker pushed on the gate with his flashlight. "Locked. Probably frozen when the electricity cut off."

"There should be a manual override, sir." McCormick ran
his hands over the gate. Then, grunting softly, he put his body

weight into pushing against something Siobahn couldn't see. A second later, the gate popped opened.

McCormick walked through first. Siobahn and Ryker followed him onto a square metal landing that formed the focal point for two staircases. The stairs on the left led up to the observation window and the back end of the final gallery of the museum. The stairs on the right descended to the lower level where the restrooms and special exhibits were located.

"Which way Ms. Murphy?" McCormick asked.

"Down."

Siobahn started to follow McCormick down the stairs, but stopped when the click of her high heels ricocheted through the stairwell. "Sorry. Should have thought of that," she said sotto voce, bending to remove her sandals and placing them on the landing. The metal treads were cold underneath her bare feet as she moved down the stairs, and she missed the height her heels had given her. *But at least if I have to run, my heels won't trip me up.*

"Uh-oh," Siobahn whispered when they reached the second landing. The hidden door to the back rooms was cracked open.

"McCormick." Ryker took hold of Siobahn's arm as if he didn't trust her not to charge in.

The man was too smart for his own good.

"Yes, sir." McCormick slipped past Siobahn.

She held her breath. *Please let Robert be okay. Please let—*

Several interminable minutes later, McCormick returned. "Sir, we'd better call 9-1-1."

"No!" Siobahn surged forward, breaking free of Ryker's grip.

"Dammit Siobahn, wait! You don't know what's—"

Fear drove her forward. Robert couldn't be dead. He'd said the museum had excellent security. That he was safer here than he was in his university's lab. Yet she hadn't seen any extraordinary security measures. Hadn't the three of them practically waltzed right in? Or had Robert forgotten to take into account the damage a power outage could wreak?

"Ms. Murphy, you don't—"

Siobahn rushed past McCormick, the beam from her flashlight bobbing erratically on the corridor floor and walls as she ran toward the glass enclosed lab in front of her.

"Don't open the door!" McCormick warned. He reached her just as she jerked to a halt. The lights were off in the lab and the beam of her flashlight barely picked up the crumpled form of Robert in the middle of the room. He lay in a fetal position, one hand up to his throat.

"Robert!" She lunged for the door, but both Ryker and McCormick grabbed her arms and pulled her back. Then Ryker's arms encircled her from behind, trapping her against his body.

"Siobahn, stop a moment and think, damn you. Did Dr. Penfield tell you what he was working on?"

Her chest heaved with the effort it took not to let the gigantic sob out of her body. Robert was such a smart, sweet man. She'd often thought it a pity that it had been his narcissistic, playboy brother that she'd temporarily fallen for. But there'd never been anything between her and Robert except the deep friendship of two like-minded people.

"Siobahn. Answer me. Nod if you know what Dr. Penfield was working on."

She took a deep breath and let it out slowly. Then nodded.

"Okay. Think. Use that investigative brain of yours. What do you see when you look into the lab?"

McCormick shone his flashlight through the window. Its beam reached farther into the darkness than her less powerful model, revealing broken equipment scattered across the worktable and floor. "Signs of a struggle," she choked out. "But no signs of blood."

"Right. Put two and two together and what do you get?"

"Body looks like it spasmed and froze in that position," she said mostly to herself. "Some kind of gas or chemical attack?"

"Most likely. Which is why we need to get out of here. Several developmental neurotoxins have gone missing from one of the DOD's labs."

"But...but what if he's still alive?" She dug her nails into Ryker's forearms where they crossed over her belly. "We can't just leave him to die!"

She felt Ryker turn his head. "McCormick?"

The other man walked along the lab's window, moving his light up and down as he searched for something. He shook his head. "I don't think this was rated as a hazardous materials lab, sir. I don't see a protective suit. But wait... Here's an intercom button."

Ryker's arms relaxed their grip and Siobahn hurried over. "Let me try talking to him." She nudged McCormick out of the way. "Robert? Robert, can you hear me? It's Siobahn. Siobahn Murphy."

She stared at the crumpled form, willing Robert to move. Holding her breath, she waited for a response. Afraid to even blink in case she missed a signal from him. "Come on, Robert. Answer me. Show me you're alive."

When Robert's arm twitched, she thought she'd imagined it. Then his hand moved and he tried to raise his head. *Thank you. Thank you.*

"Siobahn? Is that you?" His voice was hoarse and he gave a dry, rasping cough.

"Yes. Robert, I've brought help. Tell us what happened. Are you hurt? Is it safe to enter the lab?"

"Get...out...of here Siobahn. Not...safe...some sort...of gas...trap..."

"We're leaving." Ryker yanked on her arm, but she twisted free.

"Robert, how can we help you? Tell us what to do!"

"Too...late...he's going...to disperse it...through the...museum's...vents...run..."

Ryker's arm snaked around her waist and she found herself lifted and thrown over his shoulder in a fireman's carry.

"Who Robert? Who?" she screamed, pounding on Ryker's back as tears streamed down her face.

"You've...got...mail..." Robert said. His raspy cough was the last thing Siobahn heard before Ryker shouldered open the door to the staircase and took the stairs two at a time. A second later, the fire alarm started blaring. McCormick raced out of the lab, holding his cell phone to his ear.

"Put me down," Siobahn screamed to Ryker. "We'll move faster if I'm on my own two feet."

He let her slide down his body, then grabbed her hand and continued running up the stairs, McCormick hot on their heels. She could see the landing and the metal gate into the gift shop. Almost—

A fire containment door slammed down across the edge of the landing, blocking them from reaching the exit. Their group ground to a halt.

"There's no cell signal, sir," McCormick reported. "Someone must have activated a jammer."

"All right," Ryker said. "Ethan will have help already en route, and by pulling the fire alarm we'll get additional assistance from the fire department. Now, which way should we go? Up or down?"

"Ms. Murphy, do you know where the HVAC unit is located?" McCormick asked. He didn't even sound winded. "Roof or basement?"

She shook her head, then realized that in the darkness, with the flashlight beams all pointing away, McCormick probably couldn't see the gesture. "I don't know. I never saw it."

"Odds are better up," Ryker said. "McCormick?"

"Agreed, sir."

All three of their flashlight beams converged on the fire door that prevented them from accessing the landing. Damn it. They were so close. Siobahn eyed the upper staircase, calculating the distance. Maybe—

Ryker walked up a few steps, stopping at the narrowest point between the staircases. "We'll go up here." He turned off his flashlight. "A boost, please, McCormick."

Ryker climbed onto the railing.

"What the hell are you doing?" Siobahn demanded. Even with Ryker's height, he could only just touch the other railing. There was no way he could gain enough momentum to pull himself over.

"Watch," McCormick said. He cupped his hands. Ryker placed his right foot in McCormick's hands, then the younger man heaved. Riding the momentum of the boost, Ryker swung his body up and over the opposite railing and landed lightly on his feet.

The move reminded Siobahn of a gymnast on the vaulting horse. She whistled in appreciation.

"He's still got what it takes," McCormick said with an appreciative shake of his head.

"Quickly now," Ryker called down. "McCormick will give you a lift and I'll swing you over."

Thankful she'd chosen a pantsuit this morning, Siobahn let McCormick help her onto the railing. Then she reached up for Ryker's outstretched arms. Being so much shorter than him, she barely managed to interlock her fingers with his.

"Ready, ma'am?"

She gulped. "Yes." She stepped into McCormick's waiting hands and he boosted her up while Ryker pulled her over the railing.

The second her feet met the other staircase, Ryker put his hand on her lower back and urged her up the stairs. "But—"

A thud behind her indicated that McCormick had made it

up and over the railing without anyone's help. Show off.

"Faster!" he called.

Siobahn didn't know what had alarmed McCormick, but she obeyed anyway, pounding up the stairs. By the time they reached the top level and the back entrance into the galleries, her lungs were burning.

"Do you feel that?" McCormick demanded. "Air is circulating again."

Oh, God, he was right. There'd been no push of air out of the vents when they'd arrived, but now she could feel the faint draft from above. Siobahn shivered. Once, she'd been on assignment to investigate rumors of a chemical weapons attack in an area of the Middle East. When she'd reached the site three days later, she'd discovered that no one had cleared the bodies away. For months her nightmares had replayed in vivid detail that horrible walk as she'd followed her guide along the rows upon rows of chemically burned corpses. Her choppy breathing, filtered through her gas mask, had provided a sinister soundtrack.

She didn't want to end up like one of those corpses.

Ryker stopped. "Here," he said, handing his handkerchief to Siobahn. "Tie this over your nose and mouth."

Slapping away his hand, Siobahn dug in her purse. "These are better." She pulled out a stack of triangular, medical protective masks and thrust one at McCormick and a second one at Ryker.

Ryker shot her an inquisitive glance as he slipped the elastic bands over his ears.

"The newspaper just went through our annual emergency procedures drill," she said as she followed suit. "One of the topics we covered was being prepared in the case of airborne toxins. Given what I've been investigating recently, it seemed a good idea to carry a few masks with me."

Not that the masks would offer complete protection against

nerve gas, but they were better than nothing.

"That's the last time I complain about women and their ginormous purses." McCormick's wry comment was muffled by his mask.

"All right," Ryker said. "We need to find either a window or an exit that leads to a fire escape."

Moving slowly, the three searched the walls for any way to escape. Now that they'd stopped running, Siobahn realized that the burning in her lungs wasn't entirely due to exertion. "Ryker," she began, then was overtaken by a bout of coughing.

"I know, sweetheart. Don't talk. Take shallow breaths. We're going to find a way out of here."

Right. His employees called him a miracle worker. But she'd be damned if she could figure out how he was going to get them through this. Even if an SSU team was on its way, she didn't think they'd reach them in time.

As she suffered through another bout of coughing, she continued to look for an escape route. According to her memories, there should have been an emergency exit just past the top of the stairs and before the back door to the gallery, but all she saw was smooth wall.

They worked their way into the gallery. Glass display cases that appeared harmless during the day took on a sinister cast in the pale light thrown by their flashlights. She kept expecting one of the cases to explode, covering them with glass shards and letting loose a visible cloud of noxious gas.

A few steps later, Siobahn could no longer deny that it was becoming noticeably harder to breathe. The air now stung as it entered her lungs, making her cough harder.

She swung her flashlight around with increased desperation.

Ahead of her, Ryker pulled his phone out of his pocket. Siobahn hoped they'd moved out of the jammer's range and had cell signal again. Ryker glanced at the display, raised his head and looked around the gallery, then nodded toward a video room on the left. Siobahn started to follow him, but her feet felt sluggish. Oh, God. She didn't want to end up like poor Robert, curled up on herself just waiting to die.

A small cry of fear escaped her lips. Ryker spun around and put his arm around her waist. She felt a moment of resentment that once again she was the victim while Ryker was the super hero saving the day, then he stumbled.

Her heart lurched into her throat. Bracing her arm against the wall, she helped them both regain their balance.

To her right, she saw McCormick sway.

"Down," she muttered. "Air will be slightly clearer down." And with Ryker and McCormick so much taller than she, they were getting the gas first. She tugged Ryker and motioned to McCormick until all three of them were crawling.

Ryker pointed to the faint outline of a door to the right of the video screen. It couldn't be more than twenty feet away, but Siobahn's lungs were on fire. Her muscles constricted and it took every ounce of willpower not to scream as she forced herself to keep moving.

Just...a few...more...feet...

Her arms gave out and she collapsed onto her belly. Oh, God, her body was one giant charley horse, the spasm so painful she couldn't hold back her scream.

Ryker reached back for her, but with a jerk his hand curled into a claw and he, too, dropped to the ground.

Tears wet Siobahn's face, providing slight relief against the burning agony hardening her muscles. They were going to die here. So close to freedom. She tried to hold Ryker's gaze, but the pain had her squeezing her eyes shut, waiting for the end.

A loud crack, a boom, and then the sweet scent of fresh air touched the edges of Siobahn's slipping consciousness.

The last thing she heard was someone shouting, "Found them, sir!"

CHAPTER TEN

Four days later, Siobahn checked her secure email from one of the SSU's safe houses. Taking a deep breath, she felt so grateful that inhaling no longer burned, she nearly cried. Those first twenty-four hours in the hospital had been excruciating. She'd drifted in and out of consciousness while the doctors struggled to find something that would counteract the toxin in their systems. It had been Ryker's gasped suggestion to call the DOD that had resulted in a counteragent being sent over so that the proper treatment could begin.

Thanks to Ethan's call, an SSU team had already been en route to the museum when Robert had warned them of the poison gas. The cell phone jammer's signal had no longer been active by the time Siobahn and the others reached the top floor —apparently the battery had died—so Ryker had succeeded in shooting off a text apprising his team of the situation and asking for the floor plan to help them get out. The team had then used the GPS trackers in the phones Ryker and McCormick carried to locate them. With help from the fire department, the SSU agents had breached the emergency exit from the outside, then dragged Siobahn and the others into the fresh air. They'd reached the hospital just in time to prevent permanent damage.

Robert, unfortunately, had been dead when the SSU team found him. Further back in the lab, the SSU team had also found the body of the FBI agent assigned to protect Robert.

Her friend's last words had indicated that he'd sent Siobahn information on his discovery. Today was the first time she'd felt strong enough to log on and check her email since getting out of the hospital.

The fact that Siobahn hadn't seen Ryker since she awoke without pain twenty-four hours ago was something she refused to dwell on. He'd left her a voicemail explaining that he had work to do and wouldn't be available for a while. She'd listened to the message multiple times, just to hear his voice. Despite his warning, he'd also managed to send a couple of "I miss you" texts.

While Siobahn wished he'd managed time to stop by, she understood that Ryker had a complex organization to run. He had responsibilities. Heck, the nurses had been only too happy to share the information that, against the doctor's orders, Ryker had returned to work the instant they removed his ventilator. The nurses had also told Siobahn that Ryker had stopped by her room while she'd still been unconscious. He'd apparently stayed a long time by her bedside holding her hand, which news made her tear up with happiness.

Yeah, a strange side effect of the gas attack was that she'd become overly emotional. Go figure.

Siobahn took a drink of water to soothe her still tender throat. Returning to work was the last thing she wanted. To her delight and complete surprise her mentor, David Glenn, who'd retired six months ago, had stepped up and offered to oversee the investigative team while Siobahn recovered. She'd been so grateful, she'd cried. Again.

Once she was cleared to return to work, her first task was

going to be convincing David to permanently take her job. She had a feeling that he wouldn't put up much of a fight. The excitement she'd heard in his voice when he'd promised her that he'd take good care of her people made her suspect that retirement wasn't sitting well with him.

For now she was just grateful to be alive and to be temporarily relieved of her duties. She knew she needed to address her lack of enthusiasm, but not until after this situation was resolved.

After logging in to her secure email account, she quickly located Robert's email. Two files were attached. One contained photos of slides and beakers, with little Post-It notes indicating the contents of each container. The other file was a detailed report of his findings.

She skimmed through his summation of the scientific evidence regarding the unknown substance he'd found in President MacAdam's blood supply. Based on Robert's finding, he suspected that the substance in the President's blood had not only killed him, but had also been a weaponized compound delivered as a gas.

Given the extreme security measures surrounding MacAdam, Siobahn suspected that only a few people would have had the access necessary to carry off the murder. Robert hadn't even been told whose remains he was analyzing until the samples had been delivered by a team of Secret Service and FBI agents.

Shortly after Robert had turned in his preliminary report to the investigative team, he'd sensed that someone was following him. So he'd holed up in the museum and continued to run tests, trying to pinpoint the unidentifiable substance.

Tears welled up in Siobahn's eyes. Robert had died without even discovering who had killed the President. He'd suspected foul play and had figured out how, but not who.

"Toby!" Siobahn called, then rolled her eyes as Faith made a shushing gesture and took her phone call into the other room. As a precautionary measure, Faith and Toby had also been pulled into the safe house. "Do you know what happened to the other scientists who were given MacAdam's tissue and blood samples to analyze?" Siobahn asked.

The one good thing that had come of the drama at the museum was that she no longer had to hide the fact that she'd been investigating the death of MacAdam. Of course, she was also supposed to have dropped the investigation by now. But if Ryker didn't have the nerve or the time to tell her in person to give up her research, she sure wasn't going to obey an order passed on via a weary McCormick.

Toby and Faith had finally broken their silence and given Siobahn access to their complete notes. According to Toby, she'd been right when she'd suspected the rumored attack tied back to the death of MacAdam's son. The President had planned an attack against an island in the South Pacific, intending to wipe out the home villages of the men he believed had killed his son. Toby had also confirmed that he'd been one of the enhanced Kerberos soldiers assigned to carry out the attack on the anniversary of the boy's death. Thanks to data provided by Faith's lover—a former CIA agent and Kerberos employee who'd decided to take down Jamieson and Kaufmann for personal reasons—the SSU had stopped the attack. MacAdam had been arrested and placed under secretive house arrest. His voluntary resignation had been a lie.

Both Jamieson and Kaufmann had ended up in custody. Toby and the other surviving victims of Kaufmann had been taken to the SSU lab where doctors had been able to reverse most of the damage done.

Unfortunately, Dr. Montague, the doctor who'd made such progress counteracting the effects of Kaufmann's drugs, had been critically injured during the fight in the South Pacific. She'd actually died for a few minutes before SSU agent Kai

Paterson, her co-leader on the medical team, had found the antidote to the poison in her system. Dr. Montague had eventually made a full recovery and returned to work, overseeing the last of Toby's progress.

The full details of Kaufmann's program had also been in the SSU reports Toby had shown Siobahn. After reading the accounts of torture and brainwashing that Kaufmann had carried out in the name of science, nausea churned in her belly. The fact that Kaufmann had succeeded in creating mind-controlled soldiers terrified her. And it saddened her that President MacAdam had been so consumed by his grief that he'd been willing to use such soldiers to attack thousands of innocent people.

Still, she felt smug knowing that she'd correctly connected Kaufmann, Jamieson and MacAdam. Now she intended to find out who had authorized the deaths of all three men.

"Um," came Toby's delayed response. "I don't know."

"Well find out, would you?" The safe house had a secure broadband connection that allowed them to surf the Internet without the danger of being tracked.

"Yes, ma'am." Ah, she liked that. *Wonder what it would take to get Ryker to yes ma'am me?* Her skin flushed as she entertained X-rated visions of what she'd do if she could order Ryker around in the bedroom.

Shaking her head, she refocused on her job. Now that she had access to the data Toby and Faith had collected, she had a deeper appreciation of just how complex and widespread Kerberos's contamination had been. She suspected that someone high up in the government had ordered the men's deaths as a way to cover up his or her own involvement. But for the life of her—ugh, she'd never use that phrase lightly again— she couldn't figure out who.

"Okay, Siobahn," Toby said two hours later, walking into the study where she'd set up a temporary office. "We've got one heart attack, one car accident, and one missing person. Looks like someone didn't want the samples from MacAdam to be analyzed."

Siobahn drew a few more circles on the whiteboard stretching across one of the study's walls. "Does any of this make sense to you? Who are we overlooking? Thanks to Mark Tonelli"—yes, she'd finally been given the name of Faith's lover —"we know that President MacAdam gave Jamieson and Kerberos the task of carrying out the anniversary demonstration. Kaufmann supplied enhanced soldiers, created from the missing military and law enforcement personnel, to Kerberos for use in the attack. Based on Kaufmann's criteria, Jamieson's contacts within the DOD, FBI and other agencies faked the deaths of eligible candidates. The targeted men were then taken against their will to Kaufmann's lab where they became subjects of his experiments."

"Right," he said. "Except for the missing Captain Devraiz, my contacts at the DOD say they believe all involved parties there have been taken into custody. Including my commanding officer, who notified Jamieson that my investigation was a threat, then helped Kerberos's men kidnap me." Toby's eyes darkened, his only visible reaction to the betrayal that had led to his ordeal.

"We believe Devraiz provided the toxin that you encountered at the museum," he continued. "Yesterday, thanks to identification from one of Kaufmann's recovered victims, the FBI uncovered their traitor."

"And as far as Tonelli knows, the CIA piece fell apart when Kerberos headquarters was dismantled," Siobahn finished. "All known Kerberos employees were either arrested, or if their role had been determined to be innocent, they were moved to other departments." She shrugged. "Since my CIA contacts aren't talking to me, and Tonelli doesn't have current info, there could still be someone loose over there."

Siobahn started a new list on the whiteboard titled Unanswered Questions. "First," she said as she wrote, "with Kaufmann dead, who's running the South Dakota compound? Second, who sent the assassin after me?"

"Third, who arranged for Devraiz's escape?" Toby added.

"And was it Devraiz or someone else who released the gas into the museum?" Faith said, as she entered the room.

Siobahn sighed. "I hope it's just one person. Otherwise, we might never get this situation under control." She stepped back and glared at the whiteboard.

"I don't recall putting you in charge of resolving anything." Ryker's voice held an edge Siobahn had never heard before.

"Er..." Damn the man, did he have to always sneak up on her?

"Sir! I didn't hear you come in, sir."

A faint smile played at the edges of Ryker's mouth. "I still have a few tricks up my sleeve. Now, Toby and Faith, if you don't mind, I need to have a few words in private with Ms. Murphy."

Faith shot Siobahn a sympathetic smile as she left. Toby squared his shoulders and said, "Sir—"

"At ease, Andrews. I'm not here to court martial Ms. Murphy. I just need to talk to her."

Toby cleared his throat and glanced at Siobahn out of the corner of his eye. She gave him a reassuring smile. "Ah, okay, sir. I'll be right outside."

"Shut the door on your way out."

RYKER DIDN'T SPEAK once the door had closed behind Toby. He was too busy drinking in the sight of Siobahn. Her ivory skin still had an unnaturally pale cast, but her breathing was easy and the redness around her eyes had vanished.

Christ, but she'd scared him. Being smaller than both him

and McCormick, the toxic gas had taken a much stronger toll on Siobahn. She'd come very close to dying.

He'd never forget the sight of her face contorted in pain as all her muscles spasmed, or forget the terror he'd felt when his own hand had cramped, refusing to obey his command to grab her and drag her to safety.

"How are you feeling?" he asked, the words coming out as a hoarse whisper.

Her eyes widened. She gasped and hurried over to him. "What happened to your voice?" She grabbed his face between her hands and searched his eyes. "Are you okay? Should you be out of bed?"

Cursing, Ryker realized that the huskiness of his voice had given her the wrong impression. He cut off the rest of her questions with a kiss. Damn, but he'd missed the taste of her. Missed her. Waking up alone in bed the past couple of days had been sheer hell. He'd already become addicted to having Siobahn warm and soft in his arms. But she'd still been recovering in the hospital and the SSU had been called upon to help catch Devraiz, so he hadn't been able to stay with her.

"Does this mean you're okay?" Siobahn said with a shaky laugh when he finally lifted his mouth from hers.

"Yes. I'm fine. My voice is just strained from too many hours spent talking before I'd fully recovered."

Siobahn frowned. Unable to help himself, Ryker smoothed the furrows between her brows with his thumb. "Really, I'm in good health. Just tired and lonely from missing you."

Siobahn melted against him. Ryker rested his chin on the top of her head and enjoyed the simple pleasure of holding her. Then he cleared his throat and directed his mind back to business. "I'm noticing a pattern here, Ms. Murphy," he chided, setting her away from him. "Once again you didn't answer my question."

Her frown morphed into a cheeky smile. "I'm doing well,

thank you. But I don't suppose that's the real reason you came calling."

"No." He glanced over at the whiteboard and sighed. "You do realize that there are dozens of qualified professionals who are working diligently to make certain the last of Jamieson's co-conspirators and sympathizers are rounded up?"

She shrugged. "What can I say? I have trouble letting go of an investigation once I start."

"Technically, you're not authorized to know even half of what I heard you discussing before I showed up." He held up a hand when she started to interrupt.

"No, I don't care about that. What I do care about is keeping you safe, Siobahn." She had no idea to what lengths he'd go to protect her. He was only just coming to terms himself with how much she meant to him.

She nodded toward the whiteboard. "Have you reached any conclusions about who we're missing?" she asked.

"Your instincts are right. I believe that in order for Kerberos to stay hidden for so long, Jamieson must have had powerful help. Help from someone with access to funding. Someone powerful, yet able to work behind the scenes."

Siobahn walked over until she stood directly in front of the whiteboard. Ryker moved behind her and placed his hands on her shoulders, needing to touch her to reassure himself she really was alive.

"No one else at the White House was connected to Kerberos other than President MacAdam?"

Ryker hesitated. Giving her too much knowledge placed her in danger. But letting her play a small part in the ending would hopefully satisfy her curiosity. "MacAdam did have help among his staff. People who coordinated his calls with Jamieson and so forth. Those people have been taken into custody."

"Then who do you suspect?"

"Only a few people know the truth of why MacAdam

resigned. Even Congress wasn't briefed about the anniversary demonstration, although a few members—those involved in orchestrating his resignation or who were directly connected to the missing men—learned the truth. For the most part, Congress only knows about Kaufmann's lab and the existence of Kerberos. Not the connection to MacAdam. But you figured it out." He turned her so that she faced him. "How?"

She gave a wry twist of her lips. "This is going to sound totally vain, but I knew someone very powerful had to be involved with the disappearance of the military personnel when my contacts suddenly refused to talk to me."

He couldn't help his smile. "No, that makes perfect sense. I can understand why men would trip over themselves in a rush to spill their secrets to you."

"Why Ryker, is that a compliment?"

"You tell me."

Siobahn rolled her eyes. "Anyway, right after MacAdam's death, suddenly my contacts were all chatty again. Not that they had much to add regarding the missing personnel. Still, it didn't take much to come to the conclusion that they were no longer afraid of reprisal from the White House if they spoke to me."

She shrugged. "Plus, I remembered something MacAdam had said in a press conference months ago. Hinting that the United States would soon show the world its might and that it was not a country that let wrongs go unpunished. Then, when his resignation speech included a comment about his profound grief over his son's death... Well, I put two and two together."

Ryker nodded. "And reached the correct conclusion."

The approval in his eyes warmed her.

"We caught Captain Devraiz, by the way," Ryker added. "He made the mistake of sneaking in to his girlfriend's house, where a joint team from the DOD and the SSU was waiting for him. He hasn't yet confessed, though we expect it won't take long."

Siobahn added a few notes to the whiteboard. "Okay. That ties up the DOD's end, right?"

"Yes."

She crossed DOD off her list. "And you said that the White House piece has also been resolved." She drew an X through the White House. "We already knew that the FBI traitor had been uncovered. So that leaves the CIA."

"Myron Zybriesky, the former Kerberos employee who ordered the assassin to attack you, was found dead this morning. Shot in the head."

Siobahn swiveled to face him. "Shot? Isn't that pretty blatant for a cover-up?"

Ryker shook his head. "Think about it. All the skilled players are either in custody or dead. They're the ones who knew how to find assassins to do the dirty work or could cover their own tracks via poisons and gasses. But with them gone, who does that leave?"

Siobahn's lips pursed in thought. Ryker wanted to kiss her until those lips parted and let him in, but even more, he needed her to reach the same conclusion he had.

"Take away the foot soldiers and you're left with the general," Siobahn mused. "Or, in this case, someone in power who doesn't have much personal experience with violence." She tilted her head to the side. "But I'm still not seeing it."

Ryker moved up to the whiteboard, grabbed an extra pen, and drew one more box. Then he wrote a single word in the box.

"Congress? But why would anyone trust a congressmen with such a big secret?"

"It goes back to the money. Kaufmann's program had its origin in the Vietnam War. A man named Dr. Nevsky was involved in creating biochemical agents that could be used against the enemy. Soldiers tasked with putting one of his designer chemicals, called Agent Styx, into the water of strategic targets developed a series of interesting side effects. They needed less sleep and barely responded to pain. The military decided these were characteristics they wanted to encourage. They gave Nevsky the go-ahead to experiment with giving our soldiers controlled doses of Agent Styx, mixed with other drugs so that it would no longer be lethal. Unfortunately, one of the negative side effects of this drug regimen was uncontrollable rage."

Siobahn made a sound of surprise.

"Yes. Sounds familiar, doesn't it? After the war, Dr. Nevsky was contracted by both the DOD and the CIA to continue his experiments into creating super soldiers, spies and assassins. Despite the growing side effects—massive organ shut down resulting in death being the worst—Nevsky's program received annual funding. Nevsky died almost three years ago when he triggered his lab's self-destruct mechanism, burning the facility to the ground. Several months later, his assistant Dr. Kaufmann had a similar program up and running."

"Are you suggesting that someone in Congress knew about Nevsky's program, earmarked funds specifically for his research, then after Nevsky's death funneled money to Kaufmann via Kerberos?"

"Yes. Hidden under some innocuous name, no doubt. But that's what I suspect."

"So, how did this mysterious member of Congress find out?"

"The war. Several current senators and representatives served in Vietnam. Any one of them might have stumbled across soldiers under the influence of Agent Styx and done a bit of investigating."

Siobahn gave him a probing look. "You had a run-in with such soldiers yourself, didn't you?"

Ryker stared at the ceiling. There was that amazing insight

of hers. She'd nailed it, when so many others never suspected what horrors his team had witnessed.

He thought back to a burned village, dead bodies in poses that indicated unimaginable agony, and the sight of chemically enraged American soldiers tearing one another apart for lack of any other living targets. "Yes. It was horrifying. The effect of the drugs on our soldiers was inhuman. Worse, their superiors knew the effects and ignored them."

"Meaning that whoever has been backing this research all along likely knows about the negative side effects and just doesn't care."

"Correct."

"This is all very nice, but it's all just speculation. Do you have any proof?" Siobahn demanded.

"Yes, from Mark Tonelli. One of the tasks Jamieson gave him was to search certain lists of military and law enforcement personnel and choose those that met Kaufmann's criteria. One of the requirements, which Tonelli found odd, was that the men could not live or work in a particular state. That only made sense if a senator didn't want Kaufmann culling from his or her own constituents."

"Senator, because a representative would have forbidden picking victims from his or her district."

"Correct."

"Okay, that narrows it down. But you have one person in mind, don't you?"

Ryker nodded.

"Why?"

"The timing of the attack at your house. Why then? Why not during your investigation leading up to your article?"

"Yeah, that bothered me, too."

"I believe the trigger was your appearance at the Capitol. Until then, you'd been lost in the background as the key players struggled to either hide their involvement, or run. But someone saw you that day and realized you might be dangerous." In his mind, he pictured Siobahn hurrying through the group of men who'd just exited the closed hearing. For a while, that had thrown him off.

He turned to face her. "I believe the guilty party is the man who witnessed our encounter on the stairs, then warned me that you posed a threat."

Her mouth fell open. "No. Senator Wallace?"

"Yes."

CHAPTER ELEVEN

Ryker watched as Siobahn dropped into the wheeled desk chair, setting it rocking. "But...why?" she asked. "He's a patriot. An old friend of my father's. I grew up thinking of him as part of the family."

"Jamieson also claimed to be a patriot," Ryker reminded her. "His vision of what was acceptable in order to protect our country just happened to fall outside legal and moral purviews. And Wallace served in-country during Vietnam. I remember someone pointing him out while I was visiting a friend in the hospital in Saigon. At the time, I thought it odd to see a military commander surrounded by men in lab coats rather than soldiers in uniform."

Siobahn looked skeptical.

"Yes, I know. All of this is entirely circumstantial evidence. It most definitely won't hold up in court. Even if we can prove that Wallace knew about and supported the program from the beginning, he can always claim a change of heart or that he honestly believed the program had been shut down." Ryker lifted one shoulder in a partial shrug. "It would be his word against ours. Unless we can obtain proof."

Siobahn ran a hand over her eyes, then sighed. "Uncle Sheldon did ask me a lot of questions after my article was released. Told me that while the disappearance of the men was a matter of grave concern to the United States government, it was far too dangerous for a pretty little thing like me to get involved with." She snorted. "As if he didn't know that I've been to most of the war zones of the world."

She leaned back in her chair, studying the whiteboard with a bitter disillusionment Ryker hated to see on her face. "How are we going to prove his involvement?" she asked sharply, the edge of anger in her voice making Ryker wish he could have shielded her from this pain. And although he desperately wanted to hold her again, he knew she wouldn't welcome his comfort just yet.

"If he's the one who shot the CIA's Myron Zybriesky, then it's a sign that the senator is scrambling to cover his tracks. It's likely that Wallace made mistakes and the investigation into Zybriesky's death will uncover incriminating evidence. In the meantime, the FBI is having him followed, but so far he's only moved between the Capitol and his home."

"Hoping that the sanctity of his office will protect him?" Siobahn scoffed. "It didn't protect MacAdam."

Technically, MacAdam hadn't been arrested in his office, but in a media room in the lower level of the White House where the President had settled in to watch a live stream video of Kerberos's forces attacking the South Pacific island of Washraiti in the tiny nation of Salaqut. Siobahn's clever mind had figured out much of the big picture, but Ryker couldn't break his oath and tell her the missing details. On President Cornelison's orders, the rest of the world had to believe that MacAdam had resigned of his own free will. Not because he'd been charged with treason.

"So how are you going to prove that Wallace has been involved all along?"

Ryker reached into his coat pocket and withdrew a small ivory linen envelope. He tossed it to Siobahn.

She glanced down, then shot him a repressive frown. "Been going through my mail, Ryker? Shame on you."

He shrugged. "We vetted it for biochemical toxins."

She shot him a startled glance, then nodded. "Ah. Okay." After a moment's hesitation, she slid the invitation out of the envelope and quickly scanned it.

"Seriously?" Siobahn tilted her head to one side and gave him a look under raised brows. "You want me to go to lunch with Uncle Sheldon? Let me guess, you're going to set me up with a wire and then—what? Hope he decides to do the villain-confesses-all routine? Or that he tries to kill me?"

"Actually, I think if he wanted you dead, he could arrange that. I suspect he's going to try and use you as a hostage to negotiate his escape."

Her face closed down. "And you *want* me to do this?"

"No. I don't want you anywhere near Wallace." Ryker heard the vehemence in his voice and tried to tone it down, but the flare of triumph in Siobahn's eyes made him continue uncensored. "If I'm right, Senator Wallace is feeling cornered. He's trying to eliminate anyone who might implicate him. That makes him extremely dangerous. I don't even want you in the same city as him."

She gave him a brilliant smile and it was all he could do not to pull her into his arms and kiss her. "But I don't know that we have another choice. Without evidence, we can't stop him if he decides to run. I suspect the only reason he hasn't already boarded a private plane is because either he knows we have no evidence, or he's desperate to finish covering his tracks and has run out of people to do the dirty work for him."

"Or he could just be arrogant enough to think no one would suspect him." Sadness colored her words.

"I'm sorry, Siobahn."

She shook her head and one corner of her mouth lifted in rueful acknowledgment. "I try not to shy away from the truth. No matter how unpleasant it might be. I'll do it." She glanced down at the invitation. "It says he wants to meet me for lunch. And I did say that I wanted to get a quote from him regarding MacAdam's death."

"No."

"What?"

"Don't bring that up. Not when accepting the invitation. We don't want to alarm him. He might cancel."

She thought that over. "All right. We usually meet at an exclusive French restaurant not far from the Capitol."

"That's not acceptable. I want you to insist on someplace with outdoor seating, so you're not in an enclosed space where there could be another gas attack. A patio next to a crowded sidewalk won't work either, because someone could stumble against your table and stick you with a needle. How about the Washington and Jefferson Inn down in Alexandria? It has courtyard seating in the back and ought to be high class enough to satisfy the Senator's sensibilities."

She nodded. "Okay. I'll set it up."

"Thank you."

Another rueful smile. "I'm not doing it for the SSU or for national security. I'm doing it for all the men like Toby who were manipulated and abused as if they were puppets rather than human beings. Because killing President MacAdam was wrong. And because they killed Robert and tried to kill you, me and McCormick." She shrugged. "I never thought myself a particularly vengeful person, but I've reached my limit."

"And that's one of the things I love about you," Ryker said. "Despite all the atrocities you've witnessed, you still care. Not many reporters reach your level and still have the ability to feel so deeply."

Her lips turned down. "It wears on me," she admitted softly.

"Sometimes too much." She plucked at the piping edging her chair seat. "I think, after this is over, I'm ready to get out."

Ryker's heart gave one protesting lurch before settling into a panicked beat. He'd just grown used to the idea of starting a relationship with her. He didn't want to lose her now. But this was her choice. He cleared his throat. "I'm confident that whatever choice you make, you'll have a successful future."

Damn. He hadn't meant that to sound like good-bye. He really was losing his touch. Ryker fought the urge to close his eyes and rub his hand over his head. Instead, he held himself very still as Siobahn pushed to her feet.

"Oh hell, no." Her eyes flashed and her lips pressed together as she stepped into his personal space. So close that he could feel the heat of her body and smell that enticing, spicy perfume she used.

"Don't you dare go putting distance between us, Ryker." Siobahn glared up at him, her hands jammed on her hips. Didn't she have any idea how she affected him? Did she honestly not realize that her temper made him want to pull her into his arms and absorb all that energy into himself?

"I—" What could he say? He didn't even understand the reason himself.

"No excuses." She lowered her eyes to the erection pushing against his fly, then gave him a pointed look. "You want me. I want you. That has nothing to do with this situation with Wallace or whether or not I quit the journalism game."

"It does if you leave Washington."

"Who said anything about leaving? I was only thinking out loud. I haven't freaking decided anything. No." She jabbed him in the chest, the squared off tip of her nail making a crease in his Egyptian cotton dress shirt. "You're suddenly backing off."

The hurt in her eyes undid him. Ryker pulled her against him and took her mouth. With a moan of satisfaction, Siobahn parted her lips and sucked his tongue inside. Heaven. She tasted better than the finest Scotch. He explored the silken recesses of her mouth, letting her tongue dance along his as she sought out his hidden crevices.

She pressed her body closer to his and he realized he'd been kneading the full globes of her backside. The feel of the firm flesh under his hands combined with the sensual dance of their tongues to send blood pooling in his groin. He lifted his head. "You're wrong," he gasped in between placing nipping kisses down her throat then back up to the delectable shell of her ear. "I don't want to put distance between us."

He moved one hand around to her front and cupped her breast. Siobahn rewarded him by arching her back to give him greater access. "But I'm scared, Siobahn." The admission flew out of him and he froze.

Siobahn stared up at him in confusion. "Scared? The SSU's fearless director, Ryker the miracle maker, is scared? Of what?"

He took a step back and ran a hand over his hair. "Of losing you."

Her face lit up and she moved closer, but he shook his head. "Siobahn, I lost my wife and two children in a fire aboard the tourist ship *Amanda Lee* off the coast of Italy thirty-two years ago."

She made a sound of sympathy, which he ignored. For some reason his mind had decided he needed to say this now. If he didn't get it all out, he never would. And he didn't want lies between them. "Elaine was the love of my life. She filled the emptiness inside me left by the brutality of war. Then my children were born..." Despite the ache in his heart, he managed a smile. "I can't begin to describe the joy of being a father."

Siobahn's face closed off and she retreated across the room, her arms crossed tightly across her abdomen.

"At the time of their deaths, I was on a special deployment to Italy, participating in some NATO maneuvers. Elaine decided to fly over with the kids for my birthday, but I was out on a training exercise when they arrived."

His throat tightened up. "I was supposed to start a two-week leave that night. All I could think about the whole time we were training was that after three long months I was finally going to get to hold my wife again. To hear the sound of my children's laughter." His teammates had teased him about his uncharacteristic lack of focus that day, but he'd been too full of anticipation to care.

"They settled into my rented apartment. To fill the time until I got home, Elaine decided to take the kids over to a nearby island that was a popular tourist destination."

Stinging pain in his palms caused Ryker to glance down. To his surprise, he saw that he'd clenched his hands into such tight fists, his nails had started to draw blood. Shoving back the grief, he forced his fingers to relax.

He couldn't look at Siobahn. Feared that if he saw sympathy in her eyes, he'd break. Yet even though the silence stretched out and he could feel her tension, Siobahn didn't speak. She just let him find his way through the story the best he could.

No wonder she'd excelled as a journalist.

No wonder he'd fallen for her.

"The commander called me into his office as soon as our unit returned to base," he continued. "He explained that my wife and children had been spotted boarding a specific tourist ship before it left the harbor. A ship that had caught fire a short time after departure and been completely destroyed. He said there were few survivors. I..." His voice caught. "I refused to believe it. For hours, I told myself that Elaine and the kids had somehow survived. That the identification had been wrong. Or that they'd managed to get off the ship." He remembered going numb. Unable to accept the probability that his family was gone, he'd clung to every hope, no matter how flimsy. Because the thought of losing his family had threatened to send him into a tailspin.

For years afterward, he'd woken up in the middle of the night with tears on his face, thinking he'd heard one of his kids' voices or smelled the musky perfume of his wife. Still unable to accept that they were really gone.

"The media reported it as an engine fire caused by a leaky valve," he continued. "In truth, a bomb had been set by a local terrorist group, who styled themselves as the next Red Brigade. Because I'd been part of a team that had experience with that terrorist group, instead of a two-week leave I ended up assigned to the team responsible for tracking down the bombers. By the time we caught up with the sons-of-bitches and brought the survivors in, the remains from the tourist ship had been recovered. But it took another three months before—"

The muscles in his throat seized up and he had to turn away. People claimed that time healed all wounds, but thirty-two years hadn't eased the horror of knowing that only charred pieces of his family had been recovered. Blowing out a breath, he forced the next words out. "Before they had enough material to make positive identification. And they never did recover the complete bodies. The nature of the bombs and the incendiary trail set by the terrorists throughout the ship's interior meant that the fire spread rapidly. Flames killed more of the passengers than smoke inhalation. Witnesses on shore reported people in flames jumping into the ocean."

On good days, Ryker told himself that his family had died immediately in the impact from the explosion and that they'd never felt the fire. On bad days, he thought he heard their screams as they burned to death. "Losing them sent me into a very dark place. It took me years to recover."

"I'm so sorry." Siobahn's words vibrated against his chest. When had she stepped into his embrace? When had his arms banded around her as if she was the only thing holding him up?

For a long time he just held her. Accepting her sympathy and listening to the faint tick of the grandfather clock in the corner. Slowly the grief settled back into the quiet place it usually occupied in a far corner of his soul. The pain in his heart eased. He became aware of the warmth of the woman in his arms. Not just her physical warmth, but the glow from her generous heart.

"I've never let a woman get that close to me again," he confessed.

Siobahn stiffened. He soothed his hand down the tense line of her back. "Until you."

With his other hand he tipped her head back. "I said that I'm scared, Siobahn. I am. Scared of losing you, because you've become vitally important to me."

The fragile hope in her eyes undid him. He stroked his thumb across her lips. "I care for you, Siobahn. Far more than I ever thought I could."

This time the kiss was softer. Not so much a physical exploration as a promise. Ryker sank into her mouth and knew that there was no way he would let her go.

She sighed and her arms twined around his neck. Ryker settled his hands on her lower back, content to continue the gentle give and take of the kiss.

A knock sounded on the door. "Sir, we need to leave now if you're going to be on time for your next appointment." Ethan's reminder made Ryker groan.

With one last press of lips, he reluctantly let Siobahn go.

Her eyes were clouded by desire as she looked up at him. Her slow, luminous smile had him going back in for one more kiss.

"Sir! Is everything all right in there?"

Ryker sighed. "Yes, Ethan. I'll be right out."

He stepped away from Siobahn. "I'll send a team over to coordinate the logistics of your meet with Senator Wallace." He gave her a smile that he hoped held all the hope and anticipation he felt. "Expect to see me tonight. In your bedroom."

He watched in fascination as pink tinged Siobahn's cheeks. "Is that right?"

Leaning down, he whispered against her ear. "And I'm bringing restraints."

She swallowed loud enough for him to hear and blinked in surprise, making him grin with male satisfaction.

Nipping her bottom lip, Ryker said, "Hours, Siobahn. I'm going to explore your body for hours."

"Er..." Siobahn coughed and the color on her cheeks darkened.

With a satisfied grin, he turned and left before he said to hell with his meeting.

"Just for the record, Ryker," Siobahn called, her voice husky with arousal. "I care for you, too."

Unwilling to let her have the last word, he called back "Good" just before the door closed behind him.

"RYKER!" Siobahn arched her back and whimpered as he swirled his tongue between her legs. Sweat dripped off her body and her fingers curled against the restraints tying her to the headboard. "I need to touch you, dammit. It's my turn."

The wicked man only laughed and scraped his teeth lightly against her clit. True to his word, Ryker had slipped into her bedroom at the safe house while she was drying off after her shower. She still couldn't believe that she'd let him put the restraints on her. Not that she was a prude, but she usually didn't engage in bedroom games until she'd been dating a man for a while and learned to trust him.

With Ryker, however, lack of trust had never been an issue.

Control was. Despite the fact that she'd climaxed numerous times tonight, she still hated being in a position of vulnerability. For once she'd like to be the strong one.

She clamped her thighs around Ryker's head, causing him to glance up. "Please."

Those penetrating gray eyes studied her. Once again she had the eerie sensation that he could see into her soul. Just when she thought she was going to have to actually confess her inability to take this sense of powerlessness any longer, he nodded. Giving her one last lick, he crawled up her body and reached for the key to the restraints that he'd placed on the bedside table.

The movement put one of his nipples within reach. Siobahn took advantage and tugged the sweet little bud into her mouth. Ryker hissed in surprise and glanced down at her. She gave him back an innocent look and bit down lightly.

Ryker's eyes flared with heat. "Behave, woman, or I won't release you." He dangled the key in front of her.

Letting his nipple slip out of her mouth, Siobahn pursed her lips in a pout.

"That's better."

Ryker leaned across her to unlock first one, then the other restraint. As soon as she was free, Siobahn sat up, threw the restraints on the bed and rubbed her wrists.

Ryker's expression immediately turned contrite. "I'm sorry. Were they too tight? Did they hurt you?"

Siobahn shook her head. "No, they were fine. Just annoying." After shaking out her stiff arms, she ran her hands up Ryker's chest to the back of his neck, then moved in for a long, languid kiss. She let her hands drift lower, stroking over the firm muscles of his buttocks. Then, before he realized her intent, she snapped one of the restraints around his wrist.

He pulled back from the kiss, one eyebrow raised.

She cleared her throat. "Do you mind?" Maybe an alpha male like Ryker wouldn't be comfortable giving up control.

That wicked light returned to his eyes and he lay down on his back, holding his other hand out. "Go ahead. Show me what you've got."

Siobahn grinned as she snapped the second restraint in place. "Haven't you figured out yet how competitive I am? I never back down from a challenge." Sitting back on her heels, she surveyed his body. "Hmm...where to start?"

His thick, hard cock stood out proudly, demanding her attention. Proving that Ryker most definitely did not need Viagra.

"I think I'll start at the top and work my way down." With that, she straddled Ryker's torso and tunneled her hands through his short hair. He gave a bark of laughter that turned into a purr of delight as she massaged his scalp. She then proceeded to map every inch of him with her fingers, lips and tongue, until she saw the same frustrated desire burning in his eyes that she'd recently experienced.

"Okay," she gasped after she'd finished giving special attention to his toes. "I think we're even." She slid up his body, letting her breasts trail across his chest, and undid the restraints.

No sooner had the second restraint fallen to the bed when Ryker grabbed a condom from the table, slipped it on in record time, and flipped her onto her hands and knees. They were both so primed that his first thrust triggered her orgasm. She screamed his name as she came, digging her nails into the bedsheets as his own climax tore through him.

Afterward, as they lay snuggled together on the bed, the sweat cooling on their bodies, Siobahn whispered drowsily, "I love you Ryker. I know it's probably too soon to say it, but I've been in enough relationships to know the difference between lust and love. I love you."

Ryker's arms tightened around her. "Good. Because I've been in love with you since the moment you ran into me at the Capitol."

"Okay," Siobahn mumbled as sleep took her. "Glad we got that settled."

Ryker's laugh rumbling against her back was the last thing she heard.

CHAPTER TWELVE

Siobahn did not want to believe that Senator Wallace, the man she'd grown up calling uncle, could have cold-heartedly ordered her death. Or even been complicit in looking the other way while one of the other players took lethal action.

Yet the ball of nerves in her belly as she sat across from him at an outside table at the Washington and Jefferson Inn told the truth. Deep down, she knew it was possible he was guilty. Unfortunately, so far their conversation had been innocuous. They'd caught up on their families, discussed the weather and the local sports teams. All par for the course.

As they waited for their coffee and desserts to be brought out, Siobahn knew it was time to up the stakes. "I don't know if you've heard," she said, tracing her finger across a delicate rose printed on the tablecloth, "but I was attacked at home a few nights ago."

She watched the senator's expression through her lashes. Her heart sank as his eyes narrowed before smoothing into a look of fatherly concern.

"That's terrible, my dear. Simply terrible. Why didn't you

say something sooner?" He scowled at her. "Have you notified your family?"

Yes, you bastard, that would complicate matters, wouldn't it? She'd never considered that if she told her family her plan, Wallace might hesitate to act out of fear of retaliation from her father and brothers.

Siobahn forced herself to give a rueful smile. "No, you know me. I don't like to worry my family." She dealt with her own problems, thank you very much, then notified her family afterward. Otherwise, her father and brothers would step in and take over her life.

The senator nodded. "Good. Good. An independent woman like yourself doesn't need to go running to her family every time she has a little scare." He reached out and patted her hand. She tensed, fearing the prick of a needle, but all she felt was his clammy skin before he withdrew his hand. "You just let me know if there's anything I can do to help. I have contacts in all facets of the local law enforcement community."

Siobahn managed a weak smile. "Thank you. I will." Interesting, though, that he hadn't asked if she was all right. Or even what happened.

The waiter arrived with their coffee, then went back to get their desserts. Wallace was in the middle of a story about a recent party he'd attended where some local celebrities had fawned over him when Siobahn's phone rang. Recognizing the special ringtone she'd set up with Ryker, she pulled the phone out of her purse.

"Excuse me," she said, knowing how much Wallace hated being interrupted. "I'm expecting an important call and I need to answer this."

The flash of annoyance in Wallace's eyes was quickly replaced by avuncular exasperation. "Of course, my dear. I understand the importance of fulfilling one's responsibilities."

Siobahn smiled at him and answered the call. "Hello?"

"Are you having fun yet?" Ryker said softly.

"No." As discussed, Siobahn shot Wallace a look of alarm, as if she'd heard some disturbing news. "Are you certain?"

"Certain that I wish we could have done this another way? Hell, yes."

Hearing Ryker's voice settled some of the butterflies in her stomach, but didn't the man care that the FBI was listening in?

"He was murdered? That can't be right." Gathering up her purse, Siobahn slid out of her chair, making certain that she kept a wary eye on Wallace. "But—"

"You're doing great, Siobahn," Ryker said. "I didn't know you were such a gifted actress."

"Wait. Let me find someplace private, okay? Then you can finish that thought. All right?" Giving the senator a shaky smile, she began backing away from him. His eyes narrowed and his lips flattened into a tight line.

Siobahn bit her lip and glanced away, as if guilty of hiding something. Fully expecting Wallace to try and stop her, she was surprised when he just watched her walk away.

Hurrying across the nearly deserted courtyard, Siobahn kept the now silent phone to her ear, grimacing as if she'd received bad news. She only slowed down when she reached the relative safety of the ladies' room. Ending the call, she shoved her phone back in her purse. If this attempt to draw Wallace out didn't succeed, maybe it wasn't because he was too smart to act against her in public. Maybe they just had the wrong guy.

She grabbed some paper towels out of the stack along the back of the sink, wet them with cold water, and placed them on the back of her neck. Closed her eyes and tried to still the pounding of her heart, knowing that her nerves were due more to the potential of Uncle Sheldon's betrayal than to fear of any physical danger.

The loud buzz of an incoming text on her cell phone made

her jump. Taking a deep breath, she threw the wet paper towels in the trash, dried her hands, then read the message from Ryker.

Wallace seen dropping substance into your coffee. Team moving in. Stay put until I come for you.

No. She wasn't going to hide in here while Wallace was led away. She needed to see his face. Needed an explanation.

Opening the door to the corridor, she stepped into controlled chaos. Men with windbreakers proclaiming FBI on the back had invaded the courtyard. Two agents held Senator Wallace by the arms and she saw the glint of handcuffs on his wrists. From the furious expression on the senator's face, he was arguing with the agent in front of him. Or maybe reaming the agent a new one.

Siobahn headed toward the French doors leading to the courtyard.

"Ma'am, you're not supposed to go out there."

Siobahn shot the agent a glare. "Senator Wallace just tried to poison me. I think I have the right to an explanation. Don't you? Besides," she gestured to the agents milling around. "What can he possibly do to me with all of you surrounding him?"

"Sorry, but we're under ord—"

Siobahn used her shorter size to slip past the agent. Putting a look of alarm on her face, she strode into the crowd. "Uncle Sheldon! What's going on?"

Upon hearing her voice, the senator's anger drained away and a slightly confused look took its place. God, had he always been such a consummate actor? How had she never noticed?

"There's been a terrible mistake, Siobahn." Here was the imperious senator, emphasized by a regal glare at the nearest agents. "They think I..." He shook his head and his expression turned to one of disbelief. "They actually accused me of putting something in your coffee. Honestly. Can you believe such rubbish? As if I would ever hurt you."

Siobahn made certain to keep her tone sympathetic. "You're right. I'm sure there's just some horrible mix up." She turned toward the FBI agent hovering by their table. "This is very easy to clear up." She snatched her cup from the table and raised it to her lips.

"No!"

The senator knocked into her with his shoulder. The cup flew out of her hands. The nearest agent caught the cup before it hit the ground, but no one caught Siobahn's stomach as it plummeted.

She'd really hoped they were wrong. "Uncle Sheldon? If there's nothing wrong with my coffee, why did you just stop me from drinking it?"

"Why...why... I was protecting you." He drew himself up tall. "I might be innocent, but clearly the FBI suspects someone is trying to kill you. Anyone in the restaurant could have gotten to your coffee before it even reached the table." He nodded. "Yes. I saved your life."

The agent in charge shook his head. "Wrong. The FBI prepared the food today and our agents carried it to the table. No one else got close enough to doctor the food. Plus, we have tape of you reaching across and dumping something in her coffee while Ms. Murphy was in the ladies' room."

"Sugar. That's all. Siobahn likes her coffee sweet. I was just being helpful."

Siobahn took a step back. "Why? Why try to kill me? What threat did I pose to you?" Her voice echoed with betrayal. "I trusted you."

Wallace slowly turned his head side to side, eyeing the milling agents. Then he pulled against his captors. "Let me go. I am a Senator of the United States of America. I am immune from your petty accusations."

"No one is immune to attempted murder charges, Senator," the agent in charge stated.

Wallace turned back to Siobahn. "Siobahn, you know me. I've always treated you like one of my own children. Tell these men that the restraints are unnecessary. I'm certain we can resolve this misunderstanding peacefully."

Siobahn shook her head and stepped away until the edge of a table bumped against the back of her legs. "No." She shook her head again, feeling like a little girl desperate to deny the scary truth. "No. I just can't trust you any more."

"You don't understand, girl. I'm a patriot. A true blue American. My entire life has been dedicated to protecting this great country of ours."

"Since when did protecting our country involve murdering U.S. citizens?" she demanded. "Or killing President MacAdam?"

Wallace blanched. Then he squared his shoulders and looked down his nose at the agent. "I want my lawyer."

Siobahn turned away, tears stinging her eyes. As she passed close to Wallace, he leaned over. "I never wanted you hurt, Siobahn. Please believe that. You're like a daughter to me."

Her throat tightened, cutting off her air for a moment. Choking, she pushed through the crowd of agents into the main restaurant. Only when she reached the relative quiet of the dining room was she able to take a deep breath.

Her knees gave out and she sank into the nearest chair. Then she put her head in her hands and wept.

At some point she registered that she wasn't alone. Ryker's familiar soap-and-aftershave scent identified him without forcing her to lift her tear stained face. When she finally raised her head, she discovered that they were alone in the restaurant. Through the window she saw a few agents lingering in the courtyard, but everyone else had left.

"I'm sorry, Siobahn. I wish it could have turned out differently." The sympathy in Ryker's eyes almost started a new bout of crying. Except she felt as if she'd been completely drained of tears.

She shrugged.

"Come on." Ryker stood up and held out his hand. "I'll take you home."

She rose and entwined her fingers with his. "Will you stay with me?"

He squeezed her hand and shot her a look so laden with emotion her heart soared. "Always."

EPILOGUE

Two Months Later

RYKER TAPPED his dessert spoon against the side of his water glass. Immediately all eyes at Siobahn's dining room table turned toward him. He'd arranged for the key SSU players —Gabby Montague and Rafe Andros, Niko Andros and his wife Jenna, Kai Paterson and his fiancée Susana Dias, Mark Tonelli and Faith Andrews, and Toby Andrews—to meet here at Siobahn's house in Georgetown in order to celebrate the end to the Kerberos situation.

"I would like to propose a toast." Ryker raised his wine glass. "To perseverance. Honor. Loyalty. Integrity. Thanks to each and every one of you sitting around this table for your hard work and sacrifice in the pursuit of bringing Kerberos and Kaufmann's program into the light."

The assembled guests raised their glasses. "Hear, hear." Faces broke into grins as they clinked their glasses together.

"To truth, justice, and the SSU!" Toby called out. His release from the DOD had been finalized a week after Wallace's arrest. He'd joined the SSU the next day.

Another round of encouragement rang out.

"What's happening with Senator Wallace?" Kai asked.

Ryker caught the flash of sadness on Siobahn's face. She was coping, but it would take time for the pain of Wallace's betrayal to fade.

"He is being carefully guarded by a multi-agency team whose members have been cleared of any involvement with Jamieson or Kaufmann," Ryker said. "Wallace still insists he's done nothing wrong and has refused to talk during interrogations. He claims that the packet in his coat that contained traces of the poison found in the coffee from Siobahn's cup was planted by the FBI. Even though the video clearly shows him reaching into his coat pocket then dumping the contents of the packet into the cup. As far as tying him to Nevsky and then to Jamieson and Kaufmann, the data team is making progress on recovering the files he'd tried to wipe from his computer."

"The joint CIA and SSU team assigned to pulling data from Kerberos's computers has uncovered some incriminating files that point to collaboration between Jamieson and the senator," Mark Tonelli added. "After the data has been reviewed it will be given over to the prosecution as leverage to get the senator to talk."

A smile touched Ryker's lips. The former CIA agent had come a long way from the arrogant bastard who'd sat in Ryker's office all those months ago and demanded to accompany Jenna Paterson to Moscow. Tonelli had always made no secret of the fact he considered the SSU an inferior, poorly skilled organization that had no legitimate role in the national security infrastructure. But the man's attitude had done a one-eighty since he'd contacted Ryker from Moscow asking for a deal in exchange for help taking down Jamieson. Ryker had never asked, but Faith had hinted that Tonelli's change of heart had started with his visit to Dr. Ivanov's lab. Ivanov had been a colleague of Dr. Nevsky's, running similar experiments aimed at creating a super soldier or assassin. Having seen the videos recovered from Ivanov's compound, Ryker could well believe that witnessing those atrocities would change a man.

Once Ryker had agreed to Tonelli's deal, the man had bent over backwards to live up to his word. He'd passed on information that the SSU had used to tighten the noose around Jamieson and Kaufmann. Tonelli had also been instrumental in bringing Toby home. Now his loyalty appeared to be with the SSU, to the extent that Ryker had made Tonelli a job offer. However, as Ryker had expected, the man had refused. He claimed he was going to start his own business, probably importing luxury goods from abroad.

Ryker figured Tonelli's relationship with Faith had something to do with his desire to get out of the intelligence business.

"Since we're on the subject of updates," Ryker said, "Rafe, what's the latest on the South Dakota compound?"

"As we suspected, it was an insular unit. The main purpose appears to have been to serve as a backup site storing not just electronic data, but physical samples of Kaufmann's drugs."

Next to Rafe, Gabby stiffened in her chair and shot an angry glance at the white bandage across his right cheekbone. Ryker knew she hadn't liked Rafe leading the assault team on the new compound any more than he had. They both felt Rafe had suffered enough at Kaufmann's hands. Yet Rafe had made the right decision. Sending in a team that understood the strengths and weaknesses of Kaufmann's enhanced soldiers had been invaluable.

"The compound contained a small lab," Rafe continued, "with just enough equipment to manufacture the drugs needed to keep the compound's three teams of enhanced soldiers in good shape until they could be rotated out. By the time our assault team went in, the teams had deteriorated to the point where their rages had become a danger to the administrative and scientific staff. Six of the twenty-four enhanced men were killed during our attack."

"The remaining men were sent to our lab in Georgia and are responding well to treatment," Gabby added. Since the men were in stable condition, she and Kai had flown up from Georgia for the weekend, leaving the care and observation of the rescued men to their capable staff.

That also gave Gabby some rare personal time with Rafe and allowed Kai to catch up with his fiancée, archaeologist Susana Dias. Susana was in town to give a series of talks at the Smithsonian on her excavation of the lost city of Amarinis in the Amazon Jungle of Brazil.

"Those of Kaufmann's victims who have completed our drug regimen have been sent to the Oregon compound to finish their recuperation," Gabby said. With a glance across the table, she passed the conversational baton to Jenna.

"We've had an increase in the number of patients who volunteer at the wildlife rehabilitation center," Jenna said. "Including many of the men rescued from Kaufmann's program. Our new art program is also proving popular." The SSU maintained a wildlife rehabilitation center at its Oregon compound. Treatment plans for recuperating agents and their families often included time spent handling the animals and birds of prey. Following the attack on her family that had nearly killed her, Jenna had found working with the birds of prey extremely therapeutic. When she'd later proposed ways to improve the program, Ryker had put her in charge of implementing the changes.

Drawing on her background as an art history major, Jenna had also suggested that the SSU set up a therapeutic arts program where agents could create art in order to express difficult emotions. Ryker had given her the go ahead to start the program, which had been up and running for several months now. At least two psychiatrists were present at the arts center during the day, in order to handle any emotional outbursts that might occur if a project caused an upwelling of violent emotions that the volunteer staff couldn't handle.

"There's even been talk of putting some of the art on display," Jenna added.

"Good," Ryker said. "I think that's a great idea." He might even create a piece himself, as a way to work through the lingering emotions from this whole Kerberos mess. "What else?"

"The hazmat team has cleared the South Dakota compound and it's scheduled for destruction in a few days," Rafe said. "All samples have been turned over to the appropriate agencies, and the one vial of Agent Styx that we discovered has been secured." He reached out and squeezed Gabby's hand.

Gabby's father had been one of the soldiers in Vietnam who'd been given Agent Styx. His bouts of uncontrollable rage had lasted until his death over a decade after the end of the war. Gabby had always suspected that her father had been killed because he'd started investigating who had authorized the continued use of Agent Styx despite the negative side effects. Data recovered from the raid on Kerberos confirmed that in order to stop her father's investigation, Jamieson and Wallace had arranged for the car crash that had killed her parents.

"The DEA believes none of Kaufmann's substances made it to market," Niko said. After data had been recovered suggesting that Kaufmann had been trying to circumvent Jamieson and sell some of his chemicals internationally, Niko had been assigned to work with his former colleagues at the DEA to determine if any of the drugs had actually started circulating.

"My contacts agree," Tonelli said. As part of his CIA cover as a wealthy international businessman willing to ignore legalities in exchange for profit, Tonelli had contacts in many of the black markets of the world.

"Same here," Faith piped up. She and Tonelli shared one of those secret glances so common between lovers.

Ryker caught the amusement on Susanna's face as she watched Tonelli and Faith. A few months ago, Tonelli had appeared enamored of Susana and had helped protect her from men who wanted to kill her in order to gain access to the microchip her father, Dr. Nevsky, had surgically implanted in her abdomen. While Tonelli's actions had prevented Kerberos's troops from killing Susana, Tonelli had earned Kai's wrath when he kidnapped Susana, took her to Moscow and handed her over to Nevsky's colleague, Dr. Ivanov.

In the end, though, Tonelli had suffered a change of heart and helped the SSU rescue both Susana and the chip. And he'd saved Kai's life, giving him the antidote to the deadly poison that had been part of the booby-trap surrounding the microchip.

Ryker had taken a chance inviting Tonelli to tonight's gathering. The only people in the room not wronged by Tonelli either directly or by hurting someone they loved, were Toby, Faith and Siobahn. Niko still blamed Tonelli for not keeping a closer eye on Jenna during their assignment in Moscow, resulting in Jenna nearly being raped. In addition to his treatment of Jenna and Susana, Tonelli had earned the ire of many of the people around this table when he'd left Rafe bleeding out from a gunshot wound on the tarmac in Cozumel.

Still, tonight everyone had been at least cooly polite to Tonelli. His role in rescuing Toby and stopping the anniversary demonstration had earned him grudging respect.

Toby cleared his throat. "The DOD reports no more mysterious sightings of freaky soldiers. And all reported deaths are now being thoroughly investigated." He glanced over at his sister. "They believe all the people associated with vetting suitable personnel and funneling them to Jamieson have been accounted for. Including the man who arranged for my kidnapping." A muscle in Toby's jaw twitched.

Faith gave her brother a watery smile. Tonelli put his arm around her shoulders and gave a comforting squeeze. Something Ryker never would have expected from the cold-hearted agent.

"During questioning," Toby continued, "Captain Devraiz admitted to killing Siobahn's friend Robert and releasing the gas into the museum's ventilation system. For that, he acted on his own. However, he accused Senator Wallace of being the mastermind behind the deaths of MacAdam, Jamieson and Kaufmann. He also gave us the names of the DOD employees who'd posed as safe house staff members in order to gain access to MacAdam, Jamieson and Kaufmann."

"The gas was delivered via their breakfast trays." Kai, whose specialty was biochemical weapons, picked up the story. "A short-lived, directed burst of poison gas was released when the lid was lifted off the hot dish. It killed instantly and then dissipated, so that the guards who found the bodies only reported slightly scratchy throats later on."

It was incidents like this that made Ryker believe the world would be a better place if no one developed weapons of biochemical origin. At the very least, he hoped tighter security measures and more in-depth personnel screening would reduce the likelihood that another such incident could occur. Since Ryker was a cynical man, though, Kai would soon be heading a newly built SSU lab dedicated to counteracting biochemical weapons.

"So, when are we going to be free to write this story?" Siobahn demanded.

The table fell silent and all eyes turned to Ryker. He wondered what Siobahn was up to, because she knew damn well that the President's gag order was still in effect.

"Because I swear, if Faith and I have to write one more watered down, milquetoast report," Siobahn grumbled, "that only hints at the truth, we're going to grab ourselves some automatic weapons and go join the Rangers. Vow of silence be damned." She crossed her arms over her chest and gave Ryker a mock glare that put his body on high alert.

"Hooah!" Rafe called out, breaking the tension.

Cheers and jeers echoed off the walls. Ryker grinned and caught Siobahn's eyes. She looked so damn sexy, with her dark green sweater bringing out the green of her eyes and her red hair catching the light, that his thoughts immediately switched to what he planned on doing to her tonight in their bedroom.

Their bedroom. He liked the sound of that. Since Wallace's arrest, Ryker had practically moved into her house.

Speaking of which. "If we've concluded our wrap-up." He met each person's eyes and received a nod of acknowledgment back. "Then I have some good news."

He glanced over at Siobahn. "Ms. Murphy has done me the great honor of agreeing to become my wife."

"Despite his overblown name," Siobahn called out with a teasing smile. "I think he should become Mr. Siobahn Murphy rather than me becoming Mrs. Ryan Broderick Kerrigan the Third. What do you think?"

The women hooted in agreement, while the men booed good-naturedly.

Grinning, Ryker pulled a simple engagement ring out of his pocket. The ring had two small rubies embedded into the gold on either side of a tiny diamond chip. The understated elegance suited Siobahn and the deep red of the rubies reminded him both of her bright hair and her fiery temper. She extended her hand. Ryker slid the ring onto her finger, kissed her to the accompaniment of more hoots, then held her hand up for inspection.

The table erupted in whoops and applause. Chairs were

pushed back as his men and their ladies surged to their feet. The men slapped Ryker on the back and kissed Siobahn. The women gave both of them hugs and huge smiles.

"To Siobahn Murphy," Rafe shouted. "For dragging our workaholic boss out of his office and into the—"

Niko slapped a hand over his brother's mouth, but his eyes sparkled with laughter.

"You're sure this is what you want?" Ryker asked, pulling Siobahn close so he could kiss her. "We can be a rowdy group."

She snuggled closer to him. "You're a family," she murmured. "A close-knit family that just happens to kick ass while saving the world." She looked up at him, eyes brimming with emotion. "What's not to love?"

"Indeed." For the first time in a very long time, Ryker felt at peace. For now, this was exactly where he belonged. Doing work he believed in with people he liked and respected and the woman he loved by his side.

Life couldn't get any better than this.

Thank you for spending time with Ryker and Siobahn. I hope you enjoyed reading *Aftermath* as much as I enjoyed writing it! Washington, DC is one of my favorite cities and I had a blast setting a story there. The museum at the end of the book is loosely based on the Crime Museum, which I highly recommend visiting if you have the chance.

It took a long time for me to find the perfect heroine for Ryker. But as soon as Siobahn showed up in *Payback*, I knew she was the lady for him.

Their story concludes the SSU series. However, I love the characters so much that there's always the possibility that we'll see short slice of life pieces in the future.

Finally, if you enjoyed reading *Aftermath*, please consider recommending it to family, friends, and anyone else you think might be interested in Ryker and Siobahn's adventures. Leaving a review on the retail store where you purchased it or on Goodreads will also help other readers discover *Aftermath*.

Thank you for your support!

If you like action-packed romantic thrillers that take place in foreign locations, then check out *WAR: Disruption,* the first book in my WAR series, which takes place in West Africa, where I lived for a time.

Happy reading!

Vanessa

AFTERMATH ACKNOWLEDGMENTS

Once again, I need to thank Stacy Finz at the *San Francisco Chronicle* for her assistance with the journalism aspects of this story, and Valerie Susan Hayward and Angela Pike for applying their editing and proofreading skills to the manuscript. Any remaining mistakes are entirely my fault.

Thanks also to Frauke Spanuth of Croco Designs for creating another awesome cover.

Most of all, my continuing gratitude goes out to all of the readers who have made this series a success. Thank you!

UNDERCOVER
THE SURGICAL STRIKE UNIT - A PREQUEL NOVELLA

PROLOGUE

Nineteen-year-old Niko Andros stepped out of the state prison, startling as the gate closed with a loud clang. Spotting a black town car parked at the far end of the otherwise empty street, Niko started walking. Nerves cramped his guts, drowning the joy of being free for the first time in a year.

"You don't have to do this," his father had told him last week.

Niko had fought back the tears that threatened to unman him. He didn't understand how Pop could not want vengeance for the drive-by shooting that had left him in a wheelchair. All Niko had dreamed of since that day six years ago had been taking on Mexican crime lord, Jaime Alvarez, and making him pay for ruining his father's life. Hell, Alvarez had been harassing his family before Niko was born. A distant cousin of his mother's, Alvarez had never forgiven her for joining forces with Niko's father and uncle, both DEA agents. The resulting law enforcement raid against the Alvarez cartel holdings had resulted in the death of Alvarez's older brother.

The crime lord had been out for revenge ever since.

Alvarez had sent men to rough up Niko's father before, but

the shooting had been an escalation in violence. The gang members responsible had eventually been arrested, but that hadn't hurt Alvarez. For the next several years, the crime lord's men had continued to carry out occasional attacks against Niko's extended family. The unpredictability of the attacks only added to the strain on the family as it struggled to adapt to the aftermath of his father's injury.

Alvarez even contacted Niko secretly, offering to stop the attacks if Niko joined the crime lord's organization. Niko's reply had been an emphatic "Hell, no."

Despite Alvarez's warning not to talk to his father about the job offer, Niko had told Pop everything. By that point, his father had returned to work for the DEA, although in a different job. He'd told Niko to be patient, that the DEA was working with local law enforcement to bring Alvarez down.

For a while the collaboration actually worked. The police rounded up most of the men and teenagers responsible for carrying out the various attacks against Niko's family, resulting in a period of relative peace.

Then, during Niko's junior year of high school, someone had planted explosives in his father's car. A police dog detected the explosives before they detonated, but the incident had terrified Niko. In his mind, the DEA and the cops had failed to stop Alvarez. That left the job to Niko.

Deciding that the best way to take down the crime lord was from the other side of the law, Niko returned to his rebellious ways, channeling his anger into conflicts with the ineffective cops.

Of course, it didn't take his father long to catch on. Or for Alvarez to make another job offer. After enduring a long lecture from his father, Niko had stated his intent to accept the crime lord's offer and work to bring down Alvarez's organization from within.

Yet even with the continued threats, Pop hadn't wanted

Niko to make such a sacrifice and they'd argued bitterly. When Pop finally accepted that Niko wouldn't change his mind, he brought in another DEA agent, who agreed to monitor Niko as an unofficial confidential informant. But first the DEA would work to help Niko establish his reputation as a good kid gone bad. Niko promised to continue to reject Alvarez's job offers until after he'd graduated from high school.

But Pop had never given up trying to change Niko's mind. He'd even tried to talk Niko out of it during their conversation last week.

"Nikolos," his father had said in his native Greek, "this is a very dangerous endeavor you are undertaking."

Niko had stared blindly at a spot on the wall of the prison's visitor's room, unable to speak past the lump in his throat. He knew the risks and was terrified of what might happen to him. But he couldn't turn away from his revenge.

"You think you understand a man like Alvarez," his father had continued, "but you are still young. Those punk kids who carried out the attacks against me are babies compared to the ruthless men who work for Alvarez. As I have said before, some day Alvarez will make a mistake and the DEA will get him. Or some other law enforcement agency. It is not your responsibility to try and take Alvarez down from inside."

Getting his emotions under control, Niko had finally looked back at his father. "I need to do this." He smacked his own chest. "The need for vengeance burns inside me. I won't be able to rest until Alvarez is punished."

"You could join the Drug Enforcement Agency. Work through legal means."

"Leaving Alvarez free to attack you again? What if he goes after *Mamá* next? Or Maria?" Niko shook his head. So far, Alvarez hadn't done much to threaten his mother and had left his sister alone. But Niko understood that the crime lord had some long-term plan for revenge going on and didn't want to risk anyone in his family.

"Niko, the DEA does have success. We—"

"No. It's not good enough." Joining the DEA like his father had once been his life's goal. He'd looked forward to the day he could fight to make the world a safer place.

But with Alvarez unpunished for the shooting and the other attacks, Niko had lost faith in the DEA and other authorities to dish out the kind of punishment Alvarez deserved. Niko wanted Alvarez to suffer the way Niko and his family had suffered after his father was shot.

Since the shooting, Niko had devoured every piece of information he could find about Jaime Alvarez. When his mother refused to go into detail about her cousin many times removed, Niko had questioned his father's father. Grandpop hated that his son had married a woman with distant family ties to such a criminal and had been more than willing to tell Niko what he knew about the DEA raid that had united his parents and killed Alvarez's older brother.

The fact that he was a distant relation to such a cold-hearted bastard only made Niko more determined than ever to be the one to bring Alvarez to justice.

"I've heard you and Uncle Tasi fighting," Niko had told his father. "I know he wants to go after Alvarez, but it would mean the end of his career. What do I have to risk?"

"Your entire life! Don't you see? Taking you away from us is exactly the type of psychological game Alvarez loves. He knows how much it will hurt your mother and me to see you under his control."

"But I won't be. Not really. I'll always be your son. And there is no way Alvarez will ever make me give up my thirst for vengeance."

Even though Pop hadn't wanted Niko putting himself in danger, he'd agreed to abide by Niko's decision. Tears in his eyes, his father had bowed his head and given his blessing, saying a prayer for Niko's soul.

As he walked toward the end of the street, Niko shoved his misgivings aside. He could do this. Yeah, he was scared. Just as scared as he'd been when he'd accepted the DEA's help.

"We'll make it seem as if, instead of deciding to work for Alvarez, you've decided to turn criminal on your own in order to become powerful enough to take him on," the DEA agent had said. "As your reputation builds, we'll frame you for murder. Get you sent to prison. We know Alvarez's got contacts and can arrange for your early release. From everything we know about Alvarez, he'll enjoy forcing you over to his side and then twisting you until you belong to him, body and soul." The agent's voice had rung with a fervor that made Niko realize that someone close to the man must have given in to the corruption of Alvarez's power.

"When Alvarez does contact you again with another job offer, we want you to accept it grudgingly. He'll be suspicious if Leander Andros's son slips too easily into his hands."

"So, I'll be an undercover agent?"

"No. You're too young and we don't have the authorization to send an untried youth into such a vicious organization. You won't even be an official confidential informant. I can't guarantee that Alvarez doesn't have contacts inside the DEA that would expose you. But I'll keep in contact with you and I'll use all the influence I have to keep you relatively safe inside prison. Once you're with Alvarez, we'll work out a way for you to send me information once or twice a year. I'll share it with people I trust, then let you know what more we need to take Alvarez's organization completely apart.

"As soon as you're in a position of authority, you can let slip some information to allow us minor raids. But Niko, what we're really asking is for you to turn yourself into a criminal. We need Alvarez to trust you. We're talking years of working inside before you'll be in a position to destroy him. Are you certain you can do this?"

Niko's anger remained strong at the DEA for not putting

Alvarez away before his father got shot, but Pop swore that the DEA agent who'd approached Niko was a good man. A friend as well as a colleague. A man who honored his word and could be trusted.

After the first three rejections, Alvarez had stopped offering jobs to Niko. Yet, true to the DEA agent's prediction, Niko had received another offer last month. This time, he'd accepted.

Niko had to hand it to the bastard. Alvarez didn't hide the fact that he believed he could turn Niko against his family. He wanted Niko's parents to suffer the betrayal of their eldest son in return for their part in the death of his brother.

It was up to Niko to stay strong and do whatever necessary in order to turn the tables on Alvarez.

"What happens to me when we finally take Alvarez down?" Niko had asked the DEA agent.

"I'm not going to lie to you. You'll have to serve time for crimes committed. But I promise we'll arrange it so that no one knows you brought Alvarez down. That way you won't become a target in prison."

At the time, Niko had thought he could endure anything, so long as he was the one responsible for Alvarez's arrest. After spending a year in prison, he knew that serving any more time would stretch his limits.

But I'm getting ahead of myself. I have to win Alvarez's trust first.

Realizing that his pace had slowed, Niko marched forward. The town car at the end of the block flashed its headlights and started toward him.

He swallowed nervously. *Here we go.*

CHAPTER ONE

Ten Months Later
Peru

THE LAST THING Niko had expected when he accepted Alvarez's job offer was to end up working the fields. He swiped the sweat off his forehead and pulled his hat lower down to keep the setting sun out of his eyes. After ten months of hard labor, Niko was in the best shape of his life. Since he'd played sports in high school, that was saying a lot.

Niko knew that Alvarez's mother had been Peruvian and that the crime lord owned an elaborate fortress in the mountains of Peru. He hadn't known that Alvarez ran a paramilitary training camp on one of his multi-crop plantations in the foothills of the Andes.

Digging a hole in the furrow in front of him, Niko waited for his partner, a man from the local village, to plant the tiny coca tree before he covered the roots with dirt. Alvarez believed that the best way to ensure loyalty among his guards was to start them on the plantation, working next to villagers who depended on the crop for their livelihood. To observe first hand how generous Alvarez was with his money at holiday and festival time.

Niko didn't let that blind him. Every cent Alvarez spent was tainted with the blood of good men like his father. Not a day went by that Niko didn't renew his vow of vengeance.

That vow kept him going through the grueling days. Every morning, in the pre-dawn dark, the two dozen trainees, young men ranging in age from sixteen to twenty, participated in military-style physical training, followed by working eight to ten hours in the fields. After the sun went down they had lessons in weapons use, military tactics, hand-to-hand combat and anything else they might need in order to join Alvarez's elite unit of bodyguards.

Niko counted himself lucky. He'd been promoted, so he only worked in the fields three days a week. The other four days he spent at the airstrip, loading and unloading cargo in between lessons on how to maintain the fleet of planes and vehicles used to get people in and out of this remote location.

"Andros!"

"Sir!" Niko straightened. What was the lieutenant doing in the field at this hour?

"*El Jefe* has arrived. He wants to see you. Come with me."

Niko put down his hoe, feeling every eye on him as he followed. Great. Just what he needed. Another reason for the other trainees to hate him. They already picked on him because he was American and because someone had let slip that he was a distant relation to Alvarez. They resented him because in a physical fight he could best everyone but their trainers, and it wouldn't be long before he could take those guys out, too.

If there was one thing he'd learned in jail, it was patience. And he'd always fought dirty.

Still, he'd tried to fight only during combat lessons. Hadn't always worked, and a guy had to defend himself, but he went out of his way not to stir up trouble. He needed to excel and get promoted out of here. Otherwise he wasn't going to make any progress toward his revenge.

A few of the villagers he'd made friends with muttered good luck in the local Indian dialect. The other trainees mostly stared at him with a mix of resentment and glee, depending on whether they thought he was going toward an undeserved reward or a deserved punishment.

When he reached the end of the row, Niko stopped to knock the dirt off his shoes and pants. Across the shaded lane a jeep waited. The lieutenant indicated that Niko should sit in back.

As soon as his butt hit the seat, the jeep took off. The road was mostly paved, with just a few places where the rain had washed the asphalt away. Without being too obvious, Niko took a long look at the valley, in case this was his last time in the fields. Even though the work was hard, the place had a wild beauty that appealed to Niko. Odd, but sometimes he felt more at home here, more in touch with the farming ancestors on both his Spanish-Mexican and Greek sides, than he ever had back in Pasadena.

It sure as hell beat being confined to a prison cell twenty-three hours out of every day.

It didn't take long to reach the main hacienda where the overseer and the lieutenant had their offices. Niko stepped into the cool, tiled entryway and felt completely out of place in his sweat-stained cotton shirt and work pants. Remembering his manners, he removed his hat and followed the lieutenant toward the back.

Niko had never been inside this building before, and tried not to gawk at the heavy oil paintings of ancient *Dons* and *Doñas* gracing the walls or the various clay and wooden statues sitting in little alcoves spaced at random intervals along the hallway.

Niko had a feeling the paintings might be of some of his great-great ancestors on his mother's side, but he didn't dare linger to take a longer look. Of course, for all he knew, Alvarez had bought this place fully furnished and the paintings were of someone else's family.

Realizing he was focusing on trivial matters in order to still the nerves churning his gut, Niko instead concentrated on making a mental blueprint of the building's interior. He had to remember that his purpose here was to gather information to allow the authorities to take down Alvarez. Anything that might help an assault team navigate the premises would help.

The mental exercise calmed him, so that by the time the lieutenant stopped in front of a heavy wooden door carved with a variety of geometric shapes, Niko felt a little more of his confidence return. The lieutenant knocked, then after some signal Niko didn't catch, opened the door.

"You will go in alone," the lieutenant said.

Reminding himself that getting closer to Alvarez was why he'd agreed to this in the first place, Niko stepped into the room.

"Ah, Nikolos, finally we meet face-to-face."

Niko had already become skilled at hiding his emotions, otherwise his shock over Alvarez's appearance would have put him in a position of weakness. The crime lord looked like any other middle-aged businessman. His thick, black hair and mustache were neatly trimmed. Instead of the elegant bones that his mother's purely Spanish side had inherited, Alvarez's face had a broader structure that indicated native blood. From the gossip among the villagers, Alvarez's mother had come from a line of Incan royalty.

Niko couldn't judge the man's height accurately since he

was sitting down. Underneath the sheen of a custom silk suit, his upper body appeared stocky but not fat.

The only sign that this man was one of the most ruthless criminals in the Americas was the coldness of his eyes. His lips offered Niko a welcoming smile, but his eyes seemed to strip him bare. A flare of anger and resentment answered that violating stare, but Niko tamped it down. He couldn't afford to let Alvarez see any of his real feelings. Not yet.

He'd have to get a feel for what the man wanted from him. Was it blind subservience? Or did he want Niko to fight him so that Alvarez felt he'd earned Niko's respect, or at least obedience?

Uncomfortably aware that if he screwed up now, he could ruin things, Niko wished he'd had time to change into a clean trainee uniform.

"Sir," he finally managed, keeping his head up without actually meeting those chilling eyes again.

"I am very pleased with your progress, Nikolos. The lieutenant tells me you have settled in nicely and have gone out of your way not to fight with the other trainees outside of class. You've come a long way from the boy who shamed his father so by nearly getting kicked out of school for fighting."

"Thank you, sir." Niko had actually calmed down a lot after his parents read him the riot act when he stole a portable CD player. He'd become a model son until the incident with the explosives. Once he'd decided to join Alvarez's world, he'd started picking fights and getting into as much trouble as possible. All in the name of tarnishing his good name.

It had worked. He was here, and Alvarez didn't realize he'd been set up.

So far, so good.

"Having you work in the fields has started your transformation into a man. However, I have much bigger plans for you. I need you working for me, so that I may send reports back to your family about how their precious boy has fallen so low."

Niko flinched. He couldn't help it. His parents had warned him that Alvarez liked to play mind games, but it had never occurred to Niko that Alvarez would taunt his family with Niko's fall from grace. *I'm sorry,* Mamá.

Niko consoled himself with the fact that Pop knew the truth. And one day he'd be able to tell the rest of the family. In the meantime, he had to bear whatever Alvarez dished out.

Alvarez chuckled. "Ah. I see you still care about the opinion of your annoyingly upstanding family. It will be such a pleasure to break you of that concern." He shook his head. "But that is for later. For now, I have a new assignment for you. One of my managers on a small smuggling route has lost his assistant and security guard. You will take over the position."

Niko let a little of his excitement shine in his eyes. "Thank you, *jefe.*" Let Alvarez think he was happy about getting off the plantation because of the status. What really mattered to Niko was taking the first step toward winning Alvarez's trust.

"When do I leave?"

"Immediately. You will ride back to town with me and I will explain your duties. Then you will be flown to meet your new boss."

"*Sí, jefe.*"

Alvarez grinned. "Ah, Nikolos, I think you and I are going to get along just fine."

Yeah, you go ahead and think that, asshole. I'm going to fucking ruin you, then laugh while you cry.

Two Years Later
Andes Mountains, Peru

"I HAVE A SURPRISE FOR YOU, NIKOLOS."

Niko's fingers clenched on the phone's handset.

"You should be receiving a delivery any moment. How I wish I could be there to watch your expression in person, but watching the security feed will have to suffice."

Niko winced over the gloating tone in Alvarez's voice, a sure sign that his loyalty was about to be severely tested.

As if summoned by Alvarez's words, a knock sounded on the door. "I think it's here," Niko said. Taking a risk, he hung up on his boss. Alvarez couldn't watch him in real time—the connection between this remote mountain fortress and the fortress in Ixtapa, Mexico couldn't handle live streaming—but Niko knew he had to keep his features schooled. Alvarez would definitely receive a copy of the security tape from the camera in this room.

Striding over to the door, Niko yanked it open. One of the compound's guards stood on the other side. Without a word, he handed Niko a small padded envelope, then turned and disappeared back down the hall. Niko's stomach sank. The chunky outline of a videotape pushed through the envelope.

For a moment he debated whether to take the tape to his quarters. That was the one place where Alvarez hadn't installed surveillance devices. A surprising grant of privacy.

But in the psychological war going on between him and Alvarez, Niko had learned that the crime lord craved feedback. He tended to lash out harshly when denied seeing Niko's reaction to unpleasant news or requests that pushed Niko dangerously close to his moral boundaries.

So Niko walked over to the small television set with video player in the corner.

Pulling his shoulders back and steeling his will, Niko hit PLAY.

His hard earned self control fled as an image of his Aunt Madalena appeared on the screen. Niko glared at the security camera in the upper left corner of his office, before returning his attention to the screen.

Aunt Madalena sat in the visitor's chair in Alvarez's office in Ixtapa. A bruise darkened the skin of her left cheek, but otherwise she appeared unharmed. Her long, black hair cascaded over her shoulders, instead of being pulled back in her typical bun. She wore a loose, white peasant blouse and a skirt made from the special fabric Alvarez provided to all of his mistresses.

No!

"Niko," his aunt began, speaking in Spanish, "I have been told by Jaime Alvarez to give you the story of how I became his mistress." Her shoulders shook as she inhaled. Niko kept his face expressionless, tamping down his horror and fear.

"You will be aware that Señor Alvarez has captured my husband, Anastasio Andros."

Niko nodded. He'd received word last month that one of Alvarez's teams had set a trap and Uncle Tasi had been caught. Another case of the DEA failing to protect one of their own. It made Niko question the reliability of his own contact. But so far, the man had lived up to his promises, passing on messages to Niko from his father during their once-a-year check in.

Niko had been trying to find a way to free Uncle Tasi, but Alvarez kept his uncle at the Ixtapa compound, while Niko had been assigned to work out of the Peru location for the past few months.

"I—" His aunt licked her lips. "I vowed to rescue my Tasi. In my vengeful pride, I made a deal with Alvarez. If I spent one night in his bed, Alvarez would free Tasi."

Ah, Aunt Madalena. How could you have been so naïve?

"As perhaps you have guessed, Alvarez has not honored his end of the bargain." Her dark eyes looked pleadingly into the camera. "Nikolos, if there is any honor left in you, I am begging you. Please set your uncle free. I—"

Her words were cut off by a slap from Alvarez. Then the

crime lord turned to the camera. "Nikolos, I am sending a plane for you. I wish to hold a family reunion here in Ixtapa." Alvarez's smile was pure malice, and Niko knew with cold certainty that either his uncle or his aunt wasn't going to survive the week.

"I look forward to seeing you soon, *hijo*."

Niko bared his teeth at the hated nickname. Alvarez, in his twisted way, had decided to treat Niko like the son he'd never had. It sickened Niko to hear the pride in Alvarez's voice. He particularly hated listening to Alvarez gloat during the recordings he made for Niko's parents, telling them how deeply entrenched in the criminal underworld their son had become.

Keeping his emotions in check, Niko turned off the television. Then he headed to his quarters. Only when he was alone in the bathroom with the water running to make sure no noise was picked up by listeners in the hallway, did he let his anger come out in a scream that went on and on, dragged up from the bottom of his soul. When he'd decided to go after Alvarez, he'd never anticipated that other family members would become involved.

Talk about naïve.

The thought that his sweet aunt was now under the crime lord's control, forced to submit to Alvarez's sick sexual appetites, brought bile to the back of his throat. Niko barely made it to the toilet in time to spill the contents of his stomach.

When finally the heaving stopped, he lay on the cool tiles, trying to figure out some way to free his aunt and uncle. But Niko didn't have enough power to challenge Alvarez yet. And he hadn't been able to make any contacts outside of Alvarez's organization that might help him.

Dios, *please forgive me, for I have failed them.*

Some time later, he pushed to his feet. While he showered, he shoved his anger, fear and grief down deep. The best he could do was stay alert and be ready to act should an opportunity to free either one come up.

One Year Later
Ixtapa, Mexico

"PARDON, *Derecha*, but the buyer is waiting for an answer."

Niko stared out the second-story window toward the Pacific Ocean. Outside, the air was crisp and fresh. Bright with sunshine that sparkled on the waves. Inside this former Spanish fort, deals were cut to transport drugs into the United States, guaranteeing the ruin of countless lives.

With Alvarez out of town, Niko, who'd been nicknamed *La Mano Derecha* by those within the organization, was in charge of okaying the deals. Without turning around, Niko said, "Tell him he can have half of what he's requested now. Once he's proven that his money is good and that his organization is professional enough to stay out of trouble with the cops, we'll talk about the rest."

"I will give him your decision." In the reflection within the window he saw the man nod respectfully at Niko's back before leaving and closing the door behind him. He knew it grated on the man to have to take orders from a twenty-three-year-old. Alvarez's unprecedented, rapid promotion of Niko had earned him a shitload of enemies.

Not that Niko had entered into this mission with the intent of making friends. Still, after four years in Alvarez's organization, the loneliness was beginning to get to him.

Despite being alone in the room, Niko didn't let down his guard. He knew Alvarez kept most of the fortress monitored, and the last thing he wanted was to let the bastard see how close to the edge Niko was.

I don't know how much longer I can take this without breaking.

As usual, immediately on the heels of that thought came the counter response. *I can endure whatever is necessary in order to get Aunt Madalena out of this place. I might feel as if each day I'm losing a piece of my soul, but at least I don't literally have to share Alvarez's bed.*

Niko's fingers curled into fists. His aunt's strength amazed him. She'd survived a year as unwilling mistress to Alvarez, when other women lasted mere weeks.

His sex slave was more like it. The familiar burn of anger twisted through Niko.

On top of that, his aunt had endured watching her husband die. A week after Aunt Madalena's capture, both Niko and his aunt had been forced to watch Alvarez torture Uncle Tasi to death. Uncle Tasi had died with hatred in his eyes, never realizing how badly Niko wanted to help him. Not understanding that Niko blamed himself for not finding a way to free his uncle.

The guilt would stay with him forever.

Poor Aunt Madalena had grown increasingly hysterical as the abuse of her husband intensified. She'd fought and screamed, doing everything in her power to get Alvarez or his guards to kill her, too. But as Alvarez's mistress, no one else was allowed to touch her.

Mistress, and victim for Alvarez's vicious temper.

But tonight, *Dios* willing, Niko would finally get his aunt out of here. He'd carefully arranged the schedules of the guards to put on duty those who were most sympathetic to Madalena's plight. And he'd found a member of the staff who agreed to smuggle Madalena off the property. Niko's DEA contact had arranged for a local cop he trusted to pick up Madalena at a safe distance from the fortress.

Once she was free, Niko wouldn't have to be so careful around Alvarez, always worrying that the slightest lack of respect on his part would end up with Alvarez taking his anger out on his aunt. Making Niko watch.

Niko closed his eyes and slammed shut the door to the memories that wanted out. His aunt had endure the rapes and beatings with a stoic calm that humbled him. He had to keep his shit together, or he'd screw up the rescue.

He didn't know how he'd live with himself if he failed his aunt again.

CHAPTER TWO

"No! Leave him alone. It was my fault. Entirely my fault. He knew nothing." Madalena Andros knew she should never have agreed to the escape plan, no matter how persuasive Niko had been. Alvarez had always warned that he'd never let her go. And indeed, guards had converged on her and Niko just as they'd been ready to slip out of the compound.

Now she pulled against the chains holding her to the wall in the dungeon in Alvarez's Mexican fortress. In the center of the room, Niko was chained between two posts. He was naked. Blood from his shredded back dripped onto the floor and slid down the shiny drain. A bitter laugh slipped past her lips. Lord forbid even the smallest detail in his fortress fail to meet Alvarez's exacting standards of cleanliness. Even in the dungeon.

"Please. Let him go." After so much screaming, Madalena's voice was little more than a harsh whisper.

Niko raised his head slightly. Even though sweat and blood ran into his eyes, he still met her gaze. Underneath the pain she recognized the steely determination that was a core characteristic of the Andros men. Sometimes Niko reminded her so much of her beloved Tasi that her heart threatened to shatter.

Niko shook his head slightly, silently begging her not to draw attention to herself by protesting his punishment. But Madalena would rather be the one to suffer under Alvarez's lash than see her nephew's skin split open under the whip.

Alvarez shot Madalena a coldly amused glance. "It is touching the way you lie for your nephew, but I know the truth. The guard who agreed to help you escape had a sudden attack of conscience. He knew I would reward him greatly for warning me of your attempt to flee."

He raised the whip and brought it down onto an already bloody section of Niko's back.

Niko flinched and grunted, but Madalena was impressed by his refusal to scream.

"He was very clear that Niko made all the arrangements," Alvarez continued, giving Niko several more lashes. "In fact, I would have expected nothing less. I have been waiting for Niko to attempt such a thing. His honor would demand he take you away from me. Despite all the training I've given him, I'm perfectly aware that he still clings to his beliefs in right and wrong. It's what makes him such a delightful challenge to work with."

"Then stop hurting him!" Niko's body sagged between the chains. His eyes fluttered closed. She didn't think he'd last much longer. "You're killing him."

Alvarez paused and contemplated Niko's bloody back. "Perhaps you're right. I do not wish to kill him, just to make an example of him. And to prove to him once and for always that no matter what plans he might have for the future, I am in control of his life."

Madalena sobbed in relief as Alvarez lowered the whip. But his next words chilled her. "Victorio, the iron please."

She turned her head. There, in the far corner of the room

she'd paid no attention to, sat a small brazier upon a stone pedestal. Sticking out of the hot coals was a long piece of metal.

No. Oh, no. She'd heard rumors that Alvarez sometimes branded disobedient employees, but she'd thought that even he wouldn't so demean a human being.

She should have known that the monster had no limits when it came to pain or humiliation.

With a thick welder's glove protecting his hand, Victorio carried the iron over to Alvarez. Another man, whose name Madalena didn't remember, brought out a bowl filled with water and proceeded to clean the blood off of Niko's right biceps.

Madalena held her breath as Niko slowly straightened, knowing how painful every breath had to be for her nephew. Her heart swelled with pride at his strength, yet it also wept knowing his punishment was her fault.

"Brand me instead," she cried out.

Alvarez turned his head and tsked. "I would not think of marring such beautiful skin, my love. No, it is Niko who must wear the sign of his master for all the world to see."

Body trembling, Madalena bit her lip and stood silent as Alvarez put on a welder's glove then took the hot iron from Victorio. "Who do you belong to, Niko Andros?"

"No...one...You bastard."

Oh, careful, Niko. If you push Alvarez too far he will kill you.

Madalena knew that fear for her safety held Niko back. Once again she cursed her foolish younger self for believing the sweet lies Alvarez had told her. She didn't fully understand Niko's plans, but she knew for certain his hatred for Alvarez continued to burn deep.

Alvarez took great pride in pushing Niko to the boundaries of his honor and threatening Madalena in order to force her nephew's obedience. It was all part of his twisted plan for punishing Niko's parents. What worse insult to an honorable, law abiding family than to have their oldest son be the right-hand man of Mexico's most feared crime lord?

Alvarez enjoyed the adrenaline rush of fighting for Niko's loyalty. She could attest from personal experience that every time Alvarez won a victory in his mind games with Niko, his sexual appetite grew. Yet she didn't think he was quite sane. Otherwise, he'd never give Niko such power over his empire. The man's desperate need for a son blinded him to the fact that her nephew would never completely submit.

As she watched Alvarez bring the brand to Niko's skin, she vowed she'd find a way to knock some sense into her nephew. He had to take Alvarez down soon, before the crime lord stole any more of Niko's soul. Which meant she had to convince her stubborn, honorable nephew to leave her behind.

Bile rose into the back of her throat as the smell of burning flesh reached her nostrils. Niko's lips thinned with pain, but he remained silent as always. From the smile on Alvarez's face, he appreciated her nephew's strength. Odd, because Alvarez loved it when Madalena screamed. In fact, the more she screamed, the easier he went on her. Yet Alvarez, in his twisted way, considered Niko the son he'd never had and took pride in Niko's strength and defiance.

The tension grew until Madalena thought she might start screaming on Niko's behalf. Then Alvarez finally lifted the brand. She couldn't tell from this distance what the design was, only that it was an angry red square taking up much of the width of Niko's powerful biceps.

Niko had kept his head high during the entire ordeal, but after a long, defiant glare at Alvarez, his sheer force of will and adrenaline deserted him. Niko's head dropped and his body slumped unconscious.

Alvarez made a tsk of disapproval, then nodded for the watching guards to take Niko away. Madalena sagged in relief, until Alvarez turned to her.

"Just because I know Niko was the mastermind of tonight's plot, my love, does not mean that I am not angry at you. You have greatly wounded my heart. You, too, must be punished."

Madalena pulled her shoulders back and raised her chin. Whatever Alvarez did to her, she would endure. Her own innocence had ended when Alvarez made her his mistress. The day she was forced to watch Alvarez kill her beloved Tasi, she'd vowed that she would never break, no matter what happened.

So as Alvarez stepped toward her, the familiar glint of violent lust in his eyes, she stuffed all of her emotions deep inside and prepared to weather the storm.

Three Months Later

SICK TO HIS SOUL, Niko fell exhausted into bed. A raid he'd ordered against a rival organization had gone badly and Alvarez's men had turned their weapons on a crowd of innocents, killing a child.

Hours later, he twisted in the sheets as memory returned to him in a dream.

Fourteen-year-old Niko fidgeted as Pop opened the Father's Day gift he'd painstakingly wrapped. He couldn't wait for the look of joy on Pop's face when he saw what was inside.

The last of the brightly colored wrapping paper fell away, exposing the clear, shrink-wrapped plastic casing underneath.

His father turned the portable CD player over. It wasn't one of the cheap models sold at the local five and dime. Nothing but the top of the line was good enough for his father. But instead of the joy Niko'd expected, Pop's face was thunderous as he drilled Niko with his eyes. "Nikolos Ezequiel Andros, where did you get this?"

Niko squirmed under his father's glare, shame and the bitterness of failure snaking through him. "Don't you like it? I thought, since sometimes you still hurt, if you had music you could play whenever you want, you wouldn't notice the pain so much."

His father's expression softened for a moment. "Thank you for your concern, my son. But I am well aware that you do not have enough money to pay for such an item. So I repeat. Where did you get this?"

Out of the corner of his eye, Niko saw his younger brother, Rafe, and his sister Maria, the middle child, staring at him in shock. He didn't have to look to know that his mamá's expression would be just as angry as his father's.

"It's not fair!" The words that he'd been holding back for the last year burst out of Niko's mouth. "Alvarez ordered the shooting that put you in that wheelchair. We don't have hardly any money while Alvarez sits in his fancy houses in Mexico. I just wanted you to have something nice, something new for a change!"

His father shook his head. "Galena, take the children out to the backyard. I need to have a private discussion with Nikolos."

Niko winced at the disappointment in his father's voice.

Rafe gave Niko a look that mirrored their father's as he followed their mother into the backyard, but Maria refused to look at Niko at all. That hurt almost as much as Pop's censure.

When the door closed behind Maria, Pop set the CD player on the table and rolled his wheelchair until he sat next to Niko. "Nikolos, I am only going to ask you this one more time. Where did you get this music player? Did one of the members from Alvarez's gang give it to you?"

"What? No. Of course not! I don't have nothing to do with those boys." His cheeks heated. How could Pop think that Niko would give the gang members the time of day after their senior leaders had shot him?

Sure, Niko had been in a lot of trouble at school because of fighting, but the other kids kept making fun of the fact that Pop was paralyzed, calling him crippled and no longer a real man. A few of the kids had even found out that his mother was a cousin of Alvarez's many times removed, so they teased him about having bad family blood.

"Then explain to me how you were able to buy such an expensive gift."

Niko stared at his shoes.

"Nikolos, an honorable man holds his head high and is not afraid to take responsibility for his actions. Look me in the eye as you answer me, son."

Niko took a deep breath, raised his head, squared his shoulders, and finally dared to look into his father's steady brown eyes. "I stole it," he admitted in a rush.

Disappointment filled Pop's eyes. "Ah. I see. Was this your idea?"

Niko shrugged. He didn't want to get his friends in trouble, but he knew better than to lie. "Some of the other boys at school do it all the time. They said it was easy and that the shopkeepers have insurance so it's no big deal."

"Nikolos, taking something that you have not earned and have not paid for is always wrong. Did you think that maybe the shop's owner would blame the salesclerk for the missing item at the end of the day? That maybe the clerk would get fired and not be able to feed his or her family?"

Niko shook his head, ashamed at his selfishness. "But it's not fair!"

His father nodded. "Yes. I understand that you're angry about what happened to me. This is life, Nikolos. Being an honorable man means you deal with the hand fate has dealt you and make the best of it. The DEA has given me another job—"

"But you don't get to fight bad guys like you used to. You loved being out in the field!"

"That is true. But managing the other agents from a desk has its own rewards. You are not one to judge whether my situation is acceptable or not. God has decided that I should remain in a wheelchair for the rest of my life, so I will accept this and be the best role model that I can be. I am sorry that I have failed you in this."

"No! How could you think that?" Niko threw his arms around Pop's neck. "You're the best father in the whole world!"

"Ah, Nikolos." His father hugged him tight. "Underneath your anger you are a good boy. I am proud to have you as my son."

"I love you," Niko sobbed against his neck. "I just want you to be happy."

"I love you too, Niko."

Since his father used the short form of his name, Niko knew he was forgiven.

Then Pop set Niko away from him. "But your action has brought shame to our family. The Andros name is well honored in Greece for our honesty. I have been proud to continue that tradition in the United States. By stealing, you have insulted our entire ancestry.

"Yes, we are struggling to make ends meet, but we are lucky. We have clothes, food, heat and a roof over our heads. More importantly, we have each other. "

Niko wished a hole would open up and swallow him. "Are you going to tell Grandpop?" His father's father was a strict old man who didn't approve of Niko and his wild ways.

His father smiled. "No. For now we will keep this just among our immediate family. You will, of course, return the CD player to the store. It will be their right to call the police."

Niko's heart froze, then slammed about in his chest until he thought it might burst free. Police? Would they take him to jail? Separate him from his family?

"But I will talk to the management and offer them an alternative."

Niko's eyes popped open. Christ.

He swiped a hand down his face. He'd been having the flashback more and more often these past few weeks, an unwelcome reminder that the actions he took to preserve his position with Alvarez would only dishonor his family.

As if that fact wasn't a constant weight on his chest.

Niko stared up at the ceiling. He'd been lucky. The store

owner had listened to Niko's apology, then agreed to his father's suggestion that Niko help out around the store until he'd put in enough hours to earn the CD player. By that time, Niko had wanted nothing to do with the stupid device. Since Pop refused to accept the CD player, Niko had donated it to a charity that gave toys to needy children of injured DEA agents like his father.

His father had also made Niko research their family history and write a report about all the men and women who had fought honorably in various wars over the years.

Niko had already felt low as a cockroach by the time he finished his research, but his *mamá* had made him feel like the devil.

"Do you know who my cousin three times removed is?" his mamá *demanded.*

Niko nodded, having heard since he was a child about the evil Alvarez and his threat to their family.

But his mother continued as if Niko needed a fresh education. "Jaime Alvarez, one of the most corrupt, most evil and most powerful men in Mexico, that's who. His older brother, Eduardo Alvarez, used to control all of the illegal activity in the State of Juarez. But your father, your uncle Tasi, and I helped the DEA and the Mexican authorities raid the Alvarez family businesses and Eduardo was killed. Now Jaime controls his brother's businesses and hates us with a passion." She spat. "We share blood with them, but we are nothing like them. Do you hear me? None of my children will ever do a dishonest day's work or they will answer to me. I have made something good of my name. Here in Pasadena I can hold up my head in pride. Do not shame me again!" She grabbed Niko's ear and twisted it until there were tears in his eyes. "Now, go mow the lawn, then return when you are finished and I will give you your next assignment."

Mamá had also arranged for Niko to spend every Saturday morning for a month helping at a soup kitchen. "In order to under-

stand how lucky we are and to see that there are others who suffer more than us."

A rueful smile touched Niko's lips. His *mamá* had a temper and all her children had learned to step carefully when she was riled. Both his parents had come down hard on Niko in order to prevent him from turning into the type of man he'd become.

He rubbed his sternum, trying to erase the pain sitting on his chest. How his behavior must be hurting his *mamá*. His father knew that Niko was undercover with Alvarez, but the agreement with the DEA had been that no one else in the family know, in order that their reactions to news of his criminal activities be real. Alvarez had to believe that Niko truly had slipped so far from the straight and narrow that he'd willingly accepted employment from his family's long time enemy.

What Niko had never been able to make his DEA contact understand was that Alvarez fully understood that part of Niko hated and resented him. To Alvarez, Niko was a fascinating challenge. Alvarez prided himself on his ability to manipulate people and force them to follow his wishes through the careful application of bribes and punishment.

The more illegal acts Niko carried out, the more confident Alvarez became that the perks associated with being his right-hand man drowned out any of Niko's lingering moral objections. Blinded by his need to have a son and heir, Alvarez had convinced himself that Niko would never betray him and risk ending up back in prison.

In that, Alvarez was wrong. Niko didn't want to spend more time in prison, but if it meant Alvarez spent the rest of his life behind bars, he'd endure.

He was good at enduring.

"Jefe, we've lost the western route through Ecuador. There was another raid."

Jaime Alvarez sighed. He could tell by the hint of excitement in his lieutenant's voice what was coming. Mentally, he rearranged the distribution for that line of cocaine.

"I think *Derecha* had something to do with it."

Yes. There it was. "Miguel, I have warned you before not to let your jealousy lead you into making false statements. Can you prove that Nikolos provided information to the authorities that led them to carry out the raid?"

"No, but—"

"Has there ever been proof that Nikolos has deliberately harmed any portion of my business?"

"Well, no. But—"

Alvarez sighed. "Miguel, this is the last time I will speak to you of this. If you do not have proof, I do not wish to hear your jealous speculations. Nikolos is my most trusted lieutenant and my intended heir. You insult me and my judgment when you imply that he is working against me. Do you not think I would know if Nikolos intended to betray me? We are in a dangerous, volatile industry. Losses are to be expected."

Miguel's face flushed red and a vein throbbed along his temple, but he wisely remained silent. Alvarez understood that Niko's fast rise within the organization angered many of his long-time employees. But from the day Alvarez had brought Niko in at age nineteen, fresh out of prison and so full of anger and resentment, he'd excelled at every task set before him.

Except for one.

Alvarez almost smiled, but did not want Miguel to think he was being mocked.

When he recruited Niko, Alvarez had admired the young man's strong sense of honor. It was one of the characteristics he most prized among his compatriots. Yet at the same time, he loved to push Niko to the boundaries of that honor. He took great pride in manipulating Niko into taking action he despised in order to protect his aunt.

The one line Niko would not cross was to hurt a woman or a child. He'd refused to have anything to do with the prostitution side of the business. Alvarez respected Niko's firm stance on the issue. Over the past year, in fact, Alvarez had divested the organization of all such businesses. Because he fully intended for Niko to take over once he was gone.

The doctors had told Alvarez years ago, before his wife died, that he was sterile. His deceased older brother had no surviving children, and their once extensive extended family had long since dwindled due to disease and violent death. Leaving Galena Andros and her children as Alvarez's only living relatives.

He was old-fashioned enough to want to pass on his business to a blood relative.

After the failed escape attempt three months ago, and Niko's branding, the man had lost even a hint of his previous defiance. While Alvarez missed the challenge of working around Niko's reluctance, he had to admit that Niko's subservience had resulted in an improved working relationship. He no longer had any doubts that making Niko his heir was the right choice. He loved Niko like a son, and the man had given him no reason to doubt his loyalty.

"And what of the product that is scheduled to go through the lost route?" Miguel demanded.

"Hold it until we find another route that can handle the extra load. You are dismissed, Miguel."

"*Sí, jefe.*"

Alvarez waited while the man let himself out. The truth was that he didn't believe Niko capable of such a betrayal. The man was too entrenched in his position of power to risk damaging the organization. Besides, as long as Alvarez had Madalena Andros under his control, he owned Niko. The man wouldn't risk his aunt's life for petty revenge.

Miguel, on the other hand, was perfectly capable of tipping

off the authorities and setting it up to make Niko look guilty. The man's initial jealousy had turned into overt hostility as Niko rose within the organization.

None of the recent losses had been severe enough to provide more than a temporary inconvenience. In truth, the police raids had culled the weakest areas of his organization, leaving it leaner and stronger. For that Alvarez was almost grateful.

Nonetheless, if the internal investigation revealed that Miguel had set up the raids, he would be punished.

One Year Later
Andes Mountains, Peru

Niko paced inside his office within Alvarez's stronghold in the mountains of Peru. Finally, after five years of hell, he'd collected enough information for the DEA to launch a multi-agency raid on the major holdings within Alvarez's empire.

He'd turned the last bit of data over to his DEA contact last month, then received word a week ago—the first time the DEA had initiated contact with Niko since he'd gone undercover—that the raid was a go.

Unfortunately, in order to maintain Niko's cover, his contact hadn't told him when the raid would take place. All Niko knew was that if he was caught, he'd be arrested and tried like everyone else.

He'd made certain, however, that his contact promised that the assault team would take care not to hurt any women or children in the raid. Knowing Alvarez and the immoral bastards who worked for him, Niko wouldn't put it past them to use the women and children as shields to protect their own hides.

Additionally, Niko had arranged for his aunt to be taken to

a safe house. He knew she felt ashamed of her time with Alvarez, and he hoped she'd accept counseling before returning home.

Niko rubbed the brand on his right biceps, still burning with shame over being marked like an animal by Alvarez. *Dios,* he was tired of this life. Tired of avoiding his own gaze in the mirror because he didn't like the man he'd become. Tired of deciding what actions he could take to solidify his reputation as a dangerous bastard to cross while inflicting as little damage as possible on innocents.

He wanted out of these custom silk suits that smothered him. He wanted to leave behind the expensively furnished rooms reeking of corruption and pain. He wanted away from the lackeys who fawned over him because they knew he was Alvarez's chosen one, or because they feared the man Niko had become.

Although why he was suddenly so goddamned impatient after five intolerable years, he couldn't say. Maybe it was just that he finally saw the potential for the light at the end of the tunnel and, like a kid, wanted his reward now, not later.

For the first time in years, Niko thought back to the day that had started this entire string of events.

Rafe threw a soapy sponge at Niko, hitting him in the chest. It was a sunny, hot day in southern California and the boys were helping Pop wash the car. Growling, Niko turned the hose on his little brother. With a shriek of laughter, Rafe darted away.

"Rafael Archimedes Andros," Mamá called from the kitchen window. "Get back inside this moment. I told you to clean up your room."

Niko snickered. "Yes, little one, go finish your chores."

Rafe stuck out his tongue with all the dignity of his nine years and stomped into the house.

Laughing, Niko turned the hose back on the car.

"That's good, son. I'm—"

A squeal of brakes caused Niko to glance toward the street. A dark blue Chevy Impala had pulled up to the curb. He had a moment to recognize the leaders of the local Mexican gang, when one of them raised an automatic weapon and started firing.

"Courtesy of Jaime Alvarez!" one of the boys shouted.

On the other side of the car, Niko's father crumpled to the ground. "Pop!"

Niko raced around the hood. Something stung his arm, but he ignored it. He slipped in the soapy water and fell to his knees by his father. He distantly noted that the chattering of gunfire had stopped and the car had peeled away. But Niko's focus was on his father. Pop lay facedown on the ground, blood pooling beneath him.

"Pop!" Niko reached out to shake his father's shoulder, then stopped. They'd had a lesson on first aid at school and one of the things he remembered was not to move a victim in case there was spinal cord damage.

He carefully checked his father for a pulse, but couldn't feel one. "No! Pop. No. Be alive, Pop. Please be alive."

Niko squeezed his eyes shut as a wave of fierce emotion surged through him. The following twenty-four hours had been the closest he'd ever come to hell. The chaos of screaming for help and the sense of powerlessness as he watched the paramedics load Pop into an ambulance. Having a paramedic tell Niko that he, too, had been shot. The bullet had torn out a section of Niko's arm, while his father had received multiple gunshot wounds, including, they discovered later, one that had nicked his spinal cord.

Riding in the ambulance as the paramedics continued to fight for his father's life. Praying to every god he could think of, and vowing to become the perfect son if only Pop lived.

The sorrow of watching his once active Pop arrive home a thin shell of his former self, now confined to a wheelchair.

Looking back with the eyes of a man, Niko recognized the strength his father had shown. Pop hadn't railed at fate. Instead, he'd thrown his considerable will and intellect into making the best of his situation. He'd taken the DEA up on their offer of an administrative job and had proved invaluable in analyzing data that resulted in several convictions.

Money had been tight for several years because of Pop's high medical bills, but throughout it all he'd kept his sense of humor, his love for his family, and his belief in the importance of honor.

Dios, Niko couldn't wait to see his family again. Alvarez had enjoyed taunting Niko with progress reports, so he knew that Rafe was in Army Ranger School and Maria was in her senior year of college, majoring in education.

Niko was damn proud of them, but doubted they'd return the sentiment. Of all the family, he could only say for certain that his father still loved him, because the few times Niko had checked in with his DEA contact, the man had passed on a message of love and support from Niko's father. The rest of the family probably hated Niko. Considered him a traitor.

It didn't matter.

Niko just wanted to see their faces and know that they were safe from Alvarez forever. Even if he had to speak to them from the other side of protective glass inside a jail.

He sighed. Maybe his restlessness came from his secret hope that he'd get a chance to kill Alvarez during the raid. His boss was currently in residence. If Niko was very, very lucky, the raid would occur before Alvarez left.

What better way for the crime lord to die than during a massive gunfight?

CHAPTER THREE

Andes Mountains, Peru

Two days later, Niko was working at his desk and scowling at the stack of reports in front of him. Who'd have suspected that running a criminal organization required so much damn paperwork? The place—

Bam! A heavy impact shook the building. Dust rained down from the ceiling. Seconds later, the warning system that indicated a hostile attack blared its distinctive alarm over the public address system.

Niko rushed to the window and saw military helicopters swooping across the back edge of the property. As he watched, one of the helicopters fired a missile toward the upper level of the giant stone fortress.

Idiots! Hadn't they received the word that there were women and children living here?

Cursing, Niko quickly activated the special link to the security system that he'd painstakingly set up with a little help from a hacker recommended by his DEA contact. He typed a series of commands into the system, then logged out. The commands would disable the security system and take down the phones. Then it would start transmitting all of the data on Alvarez's computers to a secure DEA server.

Niko grabbed his pistol, made sure his knife was still strapped to his ankle, and headed out of the room at a run, staggering as another blast shook the building. Alvarez's emergency plan called for Niko to head to the security room and take control of securing the inside of the building, while Alvarez would make his escape through a tunnel that led to a distant helipad.

Screw that. Niko was done following orders.

As far as he was concerned, this attack set him free. He might die trying to get himself and his aunt out of here, but he wouldn't obey one more goddamned order from Alvarez.

He passed a group of grim office workers. A few of them took a look at Niko's face and shied away from him. No doubt from the feral grin he felt splitting his face. Five years of reining in his hatred had formed a toxic cesspool at the bottom of his soul. Now that deadly mix of hate, shame and despair boiled up, threatening to overwhelm him.

Keep it together. You don't want to scare Aunt Madalena to death. Wait until you've got Alvarez in your sights before you lose it.

Several minutes later, an announcement came over the public address system, first in Spanish and then in English, telling people to surrender quietly. Good. His Trojan software had given the authorities the access they needed.

Niko left the administration building through the underground tunnel and headed toward the housing complex, passing a number of groups of panicked people along the way. When they looked to him for instructions on what to do, Niko slowed down, schooled his features into a more civilized expression, then told them to gather in the large cafeteria.

This latest group consisted mainly of women from the housekeeping and administrative staff and their children. "If the authorities come inside, you'll be safer in one room where you are out of the way of any gunfire," he explained. He told himself he wasn't worried by the fact he didn't hear any sounds of fighting. "If our men succeed in driving back the authorities, they will let you know over the public address system when it's safe to come out."

Niko made a shooing motion with his hands when the women just continued to stare at him. "Go!"

Finally, one of the women reacted. She grabbed the hand of the young girl next to her and took off at a run toward the cafeteria. With any luck, the raiding party would find the women and treat them as the victims they were, rather than criminals. The women deserved a better life. Their only mistake was working for a monster like Alvarez. None of them had participated in any illegal activities. They'd just been working here in order to feed their families.

Setting aside thoughts of the women's futures, Niko entered his security code into the locked door at the end of the tunnel. A second code overrode the emergency lockdown instructions.

The door clicked open and Niko raced through. He left the door unlocked, in case he needed to come back this way with Aunt Madalena. Then he made a beeline for his aunt's room.

ALVAREZ HAD JUST SPILLED his seed and rolled off of Madalena when the bedroom shook. She gasped as the bed swayed with such force that she had to clutch the covers to stop herself from rolling into Alvarez. She wanted him as far away from her as possible, even though this coupling had been more about control than violence.

"What's happening?" she cried out as the bed shook again. "Is it an earthquake?"

Alvarez jumped to his feet, cursing under his breath as he

searched for his pants. A second later, the emergency alarm blared through the loud speakers.

"We are under attack," Alvarez snapped. "Get dressed. We're leaving."

Freedom!

The last thing she wanted to do was escape with Alvarez. Whether government forces or a rival criminal gang, Madalena would rather throw herself on the mercy of the attackers than go anywhere with this monster. But from the tight set of his jaw, she knew that if she tried to run now, Alvarez would shoot her with the pistol he held in his hand. She had no idea where the gun had come from, but even though she was reasonably certain that he'd only shoot to wound her, she needed full mobility so she could escape when the opportunity presented itself.

Catching the clothes that Alvarez threw at her, she quickly put them on. As soon as she slid the last button through its hole and slipped into her ballet flats, Alvarez grabbed her arm. "Hurry. We must make it to the escape tunnel before the way is blocked."

He hustled her through the maze of corridors to a section of the building that she'd never seen before.

"Attention. Attention," a voice blared in Spanish over the loud speaker. "This is the Peruvian military in conjunction with the United States Drug Enforcement Agency. We have the compound surrounded. Please exit quietly with your hands on your head."

Alvarez swore and ran faster, his iron-firm grip on her arm forcing Madalena to keep up with him.

Overhead, the message repeated in English.

Madalena looked for a chance to escape, but the long corridors left her no place to hide. She was still trying to figure out how to break free when they reached what looked like the door to a linen closet.

Alvarez pulled open the door, revealing a sleek elevator. After shoving his gun in his waistband, he entered a code onto a small keypad in the wall to the right of the elevator, keeping his punishing hold on Madalena's arm. As if he knew she planned to run.

The keypad gave out an angry beep.

Alvarez muttered a curse and tried again.

Another beep.

Alvarez went very still. He took a deep, shuddering breath. Shook out his hand. Then tried the code again.

This time a flashing red light went off overhead as a different alarm sounded.

Alvarez smacked the control panel with his fist, then tried to pry apart the elevator door with his fingers.

Madalena used his distraction to pull against his hold.

Alvarez backhanded her. "Stay still! Or do you want to be captured and put in jail? Or worse, die when the government sets the building on fire?" He pulled her toward the elevator. "Help me get these doors open. The system has frozen me out."

"Have you lost your mind?" she snapped. She'd never seen Alvarez in a panic before. Furious, yes. But not so scared that he couldn't think straight. "We can't force apart steel doors. Isn't there another escape route?" The man was paranoid when it came to his safety. He must have other ways out of the building.

Alvarez glanced around, as if not certain of their location in relation to the rest of the fortress.

She let out a wild laugh. "You don't know where the next escape route is, do you? The mighty Jaime Alvarez, lost within his own fortress." She made an exaggerated show of looking around. "Where are all of your guards? Where are all of the staff that should be filing out of their rooms? They've all abandoned you, Alvarez. You're under attack and they've left you to suffer alone."

"Shut up, *puta*." Alvarez hit her again. While she struggled to regain her balance, he pulled the pistol out of his waistband, tightened his grip on her arm, and dragged her back the way they'd come.

Aunt Madalena wasn't in her room, but from the lingering scents of sex and cologne, Niko knew that both she and Alvarez had been here recently. Cursing, he spun around and stepped back out into the eerily quiet corridor. He glanced left and right, trying to decide which way they'd gone. If he were Alvarez, he'd head to the nearest secure elevator that led to the escape tunnel.

Not that the elevator would do Alvarez any good. The program Niko had loaded into the security system would lock out all codes but the new one he'd set for himself and the assault team. He ran around the corner and into the corridor that held the elevator, but immediately stopped. Flashing lights and a blaring alarm indicated that someone had already tried to access the elevator.

Damn. There were too many ways that Alvarez and Aunt Madalena could have gone from here. Wait. He sniffed the air. There. A mix of his aunt's perfume and Alvarez's cologne.

Grinning like a fool, Niko prepared to play bloodhound.

The warnings to surrender came again over the public address system. Niko didn't want to be caught running through the halls holding a pistol when the assault force came to clear the building, but he wasn't going to give up his chance to get his aunt away from Alvarez. Hopefully, he'd catch up to them before they reached the outside entrance.

But luck wasn't with him. Niko lost the faint scent trail a few corridors later. He glanced out the nearest window and saw chaos in the enclosed courtyard. Men in military uniforms traded fire with men wearing the uniforms of Alvarez's security forces. A few women huddled with children in the corner, trying to hide behind some potted trees.

No way would Alvarez willingly step into that mess. Too great a chance he'd take a bullet. Or that a government agent would see him and capture him. The tunnel to the administration building was open, but only because Niko had left it that way. Alvarez would assume that the tunnel's electronic door, like the others, would also be locked against him.

So where would he go?

Niko peered out the window again to orient himself. The administration building was to his left. The infirmary straight ahead. The armory and garage over to his right.

The escape tunnel ran below it all. Wait. Below...

Yes. The dungeons.

Niko turned right and sprinted for the stairs that would take him down to the basement. The dungeons here in Peru weren't as old as the ones in Mexico, but Alvarez had kept the old-fashioned locks that required heavy metal keys. Which meant the dungeons were the only place where you could access the escape tunnel without having to enter a security code on an electronic access panel.

Niko yanked open the door at the end of the hall. The motion-activated, overhead lights in the stairwell were already on. Good. Alvarez had come this way. Stopping for a second, he listened for any sound that indicated the crime lord was waiting below, close enough to shoot him.

When he heard nothing, Niko clambered down the stairs as fast as he could without falling headfirst. He paused again to listen at the bottom of the stairs. This time he heard the low murmur of voices and the creak of a heavy wooden door.

He crept forward and snuck a look into the antechamber. Alvarez stood directly across from Niko with his back turned. One of Alvarez's hands pulled on the giant door that opened into the section of the dungeon block that led to the escape tunnel. His other hand held Aunt Madalena's arm in a death grip.

The breath stilled in Niko's lungs. This was it. He had a perfect shot. He raised his pistol. He could end decades of terror this man had caused his family. No one but his aunt would ever know for certain that Niko killed Alvarez. Even if people suspected who'd fired the shot, Niko wouldn't care.

The monster would finally be dead.

Shooting a man when his back is turned is dishonorable. The voice of his conscience sounded an awful lot like his father. *You shame the family even thinking of such a thing.*

No. Alvarez could *not* be allowed to live. Niko hadn't spent all these years working against the man to see him go to jail, then have one of Alvarez's expensive lawyers bargain him out in a few years.

Niko put his finger on the trigger.

The side door burst open, blocking his shot. Niko dropped his finger from the trigger as three of Alvarez's guards ran into the room.

"*Jefe!* Thank the Virgin we have found you."

Niko sank back into the shadows, relieved that no one had noticed him. But damn, now what was he supposed to do?

One of the men slammed the door closed. Another went to help Alvarez move the heavy dungeon door the last few inches.

Niko felt a wave of despair. He could walk into the open and point his pistol at Alvarez, but either the guards would shoot him, or they'd shoot Aunt Madalena. He could pretend that he, too, was trying to escape and that he wasn't involved in the raid. Would Alvarez buy it? Or would the announcement that the DEA was involved tip Alvarez off that Niko had set up the whole thing?

Fuck. He couldn't believe he'd been so close to getting rid of Alvarez. He should have just shot the bastard without hesitation.

Alvarez, the guards, and Madalena hurried into the tunnel. In a moment, they'd be out of sight.

Okay. He'd have to chance playing the innocent. It might buy him enough time to shoot Alvarez in the torso or leg, forcing him to release Aunt Madalena.

Niko ran after them. *"Jefe!* Aunt Madalena! Thank God I found you."

Multiple explosions shook the dungeon, throwing Niko to his knees in the middle of the antechamber. As he waited for the ringing in his ears to stop, he heard the unmistakable sound of falling rock, followed by the pounding of boots.

"Joint United States and Peruvian Assault Force!" a voice shouted, first in Spanish, then in English. "On the floor, hands on your heads."

The sound of a pistol firing had Niko jumping to his feet and dashing forward. "Aunt Madalena!"

"On your knees," a soldier shouted. "Now!"

Seeing that his aunt was all right, Niko obeyed. One of the guards lay facedown on the floor, blood seeping from under his head. Idiot.

The men from the assault force moved forward. Within minutes, they'd secured everyone's hands.

"Jaime Alvarez," one of the Peruvian soldiers said in Spanish, "I have been waiting for this day for seven long years. It is my deep pleasure to take you into the official custody of the Republic of Peru."

For the first time since Niko had met the man, Alvarez appeared shocked. The look of outraged disbelief on his face as he was led away was almost comical.

Dios. *It's over. It's finally over.* Now all he had to do was make certain Aunt Madalena got safely back to the family.

"Tell your commander that the woman is Pocahontas," Niko quietly told the DEA agent that stood behind him, using the code word he'd set up to make certain his aunt received the treatment he'd been promised.

The man looked sideways at Niko, but he spoke softly into his lip mike. A moment later, he nodded. "John Smith?" he asked.

Niko gave a slight shake of his head. "Nah. I'm more like Robin Hood," he replied, giving the rest of the code phrase.

The man flicked his eyes from Alvarez's retreating back to Niko. He gave Niko a nod of respect. "Some day, I'd like to buy you a beer and hear how you managed to survive undercover so long. It takes cojones to cross a man like Alvarez from the inside."

"Yeah, well." Niko shrugged. "Look me up in another five to ten. By then I'm sure I'll need a beer." If he survived prison, that was. Based on the way this had gone down, Niko didn't think Alvarez or his guards had suspected his role. But all it took was one comment said in the wrong company and he was a dead man.

The thought of being locked up again sent panic zinging through him. But this time he wasn't an innocent boy of eighteen. He was a twenty-four-year old man. A man who'd survived in one of the most brutal criminal organizations in Latin America.

He'd continue to endure for as long as it took to win back his freedom.

Then he'd work on winning back the love of his family.

"C'mon." The DEA agent took Niko by the arm. "Let's get you out of here."

"Yeah," Niko said under his breath. "It's long past time I left."

Undisclosed Location, United States

IT TOOK ten days for Alvarez to accept that he'd been well and truly caught. Ten days and his extradition to a high-security holding facility in the United States. None of his usual allies within the legal community were standing by him. Oh, his expensive lawyer was on board, but the cops and judges Alvarez had paid over the years to ensure that his empire ran smoothly had failed to protect him. It appeared that he'd made a major miscalculation.

At the end of the hall, the door into the judge's chamber opened. Niko stepped out, flanked by a pair of guards. Strong as always, Niko held his head high despite the fact that he wore a prisoner's orange jumpsuit and was shackled at wrists and ankles.

On the surface, it appeared that Niko was being prosecuted as a criminal, the same as all of Alvarez's men. But Alvarez wasn't fooled. Miguel had been right. Only one man had the systemwide access to take down every one of his businesses.

Alvarez had no idea how Niko had managed it. Despite Miguel's accusations, there had never been any proof that Niko had been in contact with the authorities.

Yet somehow he'd managed to ruin Alvarez.

"You," Alvarez spat quietly as Niko drew near. He did not believe the guards spoke Spanish, but he had no wish to be overheard, regardless. "You're the one responsible for this."

Niko stopped. His face showed no emotion.

That infuriated Alvarez more than anything. To be treated like nothing by this man was the greatest insult.

"You betrayed me." He surged to his feet and Niko's guards shifted forward to protect him at the same time Alvarez's guards grabbed his arms. He ignored them. They didn't matter. "After all I did for you, *hijo*, you repay me like this?"

Niko didn't answer. Just returned his gaze with a stony stare, as if Alvarez meant nothing to him.

"I will destroy you. Do you hear me? I promise you this, Nikolos Andros. I will destroy everything you hold dear. Tear apart your family until your heart breaks and you have no more tears to cry. You will die regretting the day you even thought about crossing me."

Niko remained silent. After a long pause, he turned and resumed his walk down the corridor, his chains clinking as he moved.

"Fear me, Nikolos, for I am the devil that will never let you find peace."

But Niko walked away, his back straight with pride, and Alvarez wondered if his fierce words were all talk.

No. He'd been one of the greatest powers within the criminal world. He would regain that power. All he had to do was find one person within the legal system willing to bend a few rules, and he would soon have his empire back.

Then, when they were both out of prison, he would fulfill his promise to Niko.

And get his Madalena back.

In the meantime, Alvarez would keep silent regarding Niko's betrayal and put the word out that the man was not to be hurt. This was personal. He wanted to watch Niko suffer, not learn about his death at the hand of some overly aggressive inmate. And he could not afford to have his compatriots believe him weak because he'd been betrayed by his closest employee. His intended heir.

Yes, in order to maintain his reputation and to further his revenge, he would tell no one the truth. But one day soon, he would make Nikolos Andros pay dearly for his betrayal.

One Week Later

"TWENTY-FIVE TO FIFTY YEARS? You've got to be fucking kidding me!" Niko stared in disbelief at his DEA contact. He'd known that he'd have to serve some jail time, but not that much.

Fear tightened his throat. Niko stood frozen, unable to think straight. He'd been moved into this solitary holding cell yesterday, but he'd thought it was for his own protection. Not a sign that they were going to throw the book at him.

"I'm sorry. The powers that be want to set an example," the DEA agent said. The sympathy in his voice didn't do anything to calm Niko down. "They're pushing for maximum sentences on everyone involved. The good news is that your cover is still solid. There's been no talk that you had anything to do with the raid."

I can't do it. I can't last that long without seeing my family.

"Because you were so young when you started, and because you're the one who is responsible for us capturing Alvarez, I've managed to work out a potential deal."

"What?" Niko choked out.

"They'll reduce your sentence to five years."

Dios, even five years seemed too long.

"Under the following conditions," the agent continued. "First, you will assist the DEA and other law enforcement agencies in dismantling Alvarez's organization, by giving them all the data they require."

Niko nodded. That was a no-brainer. He wanted Alvarez completely destroyed.

"Second, upon your release, you must agree to work undercover as a full-time DEA employee for a minimum of three years. They'll—"

"Why the *fuck* would I want to work for the DEA? All I want is a normal life." Niko clenched his fists and told himself it would be stupid to reach out and strangle his handler. Or to take the man hostage and demand to be let go.

Damn. He really was on edge. But he hadn't realized how desperate he was to see his family until the prospect got taken away.

"If you'll let me finish?" the man snapped.

After taking a deep breath, Niko nodded.

"Agree to work for us, taking on other assignments in the Latin American underworld, and we'll request that the year you spent in prison five years ago be credited toward your new term. We'll also arrange for your sentence to be reduced by the three years of service to the DEA. That means you only need to serve twelve months."

Christ. Another year. He rubbed the scars on his biceps. It wasn't as if he had a choice, was it? But it sounded like the DEA wanted him to maintain his cover, which meant he still wouldn't be able to tell his *mamá* the truth.

"Plus, you'll get weekly visits."

"Huh?"

"Look, I can tell that you're not happy about serving more time, but you knew before you joined Alvarez that we were going to have to prosecute you."

Niko shrugged. Yeah, his mind understood the situation. His honorable self knew he had to make reparation for the things he'd done. But his heart and soul just wanted to slough off his *La Mano Derecha* persona and return to being Niko Andros.

Whoever the hell that was anymore.

"As part of the deal, I've arranged for weekly visits from your family. Anyone who knows your parents will understand that no matter what they think you've done, they'll support you and try to convince you to redeem yourself. So it won't weaken your cover for them to visit."

Relief loosened Niko's muscles, but he refused to betray such weakness. "All right. I agree. What do I need to do?"

To his surprise, the man reached inside his suit jacket and pulled out a folded set of papers. "Sign these, then our lawyers will talk to the judge tomorrow."

Niko read through the papers carefully, but everything was as the man had said. He scribbled his signature where indicated, then handed the papers back. The agent then countersigned the documents. Huh. The man must have more clout within the agency than Niko realized.

"Leave my copy with my father," he said.

The man nodded and turned to go. Just before he opened the door he hesitated, then glanced over his shoulder at Niko. "You've done a great service to society, Niko. Not many men would have lasted as long as you did with Alvarez. But you had the strength and the courage to endure. For that, I admire you."

Niko gave a one-shoulder shrug, unable to think of any response.

With a little smile of acknowledgment, the agent left the room. Once the door had clicked closed behind him, Niko sat down heavily on the room's single chair. He put his head in his hands and concentrated on regulating his breathing.

I can do this. What's four more years after what I've gone through?

Unfortunately, now that the raid was over, the reservoir of strength that had kept him moving forward seemed to be empty.

Dios, *please give me courage.*

CHAPTER FOUR

Ten Years Later
A Village in Afghanistan

Niko tossed feverishly on his bed.

They'd been betrayed. His team had gone into the mountains to speak to a supposed informant. Instead, they'd discovered a burned-out village. The charred bodies of women and children lined the streets. Before Niko's team could begin to bury the dead, they'd come under automatic weapons fire.

One of Niko's teammates on the joint SSU/DEA task force went down. Niko grabbed him in a fireman's lift and started down the mountain. But he didn't get far before a bullet tore into his thigh and his leg gave out. Niko stumbled, then collapsed, watching in horror as the skull of his teammate exploded under the impact of another bullet.

Niko woke up with his throat sore from screaming and someone's hand on his shoulder. Weak as he was, he still twisted free and sent a fist flying toward the intruder.

"Niko. Whoa. Relax, bro. It's me, Rafe."

The Greek words penetrated Niko's brain fog like nothing else could. "Rafe? What the fuck?"

He glanced around. Yep. He was still in the storeroom at the back of Yousef's father's house in the middle of the mountains of Afghanistan. Last he'd heard, Rafe was headed out on assignment to South America. "What the hell are you doing here?"

Niko sat up on his straw pallet, biting back a groan as the room spun and the wound in his thigh pulsed with pain. But at least his fever seemed to have broken. Now that he was awake, he felt clear-headed for the first time in days.

He took a moment to study his brother. Rafe sported several days worth of beard and Niko saw combat fatigues sticking out from underneath the traditional Afghani robe he wore. His brother looked like he hadn't slept for days and, shit, were those tears in his eyes?

"Rafe, what's wrong?"

Rafe reached out and grabbed Niko's shoulder. "Pop's dying."

The room spun again. "What?" Niko tried to climb to his feet, but his wounded leg wouldn't support him and he fell back on the pallet. "How? Why?"

"Pneumonia. *Mamá* said he'd been working long hours on a new case and she thinks his immune system was weakened."

Niko stared into his brother's eyes. "He can't be dying. It's just pneumonia, right?"

Rafe shook his head, the bleakness of his expression telling Niko all he needed to know. His brother was the optimist. If he'd lost hope, then the situation was bad. "So what the fuck are you doing here? You should be with him."

Rafe nodded. "I know. But he told me to get you. Said he wanted both his sons together. So Ryker helped me track you down."

Christ. Dying. It would take them days to get back to the States. Even if Ryker, their boss and the director of the privately run special operations group the Surgical Strike Unit, managed one of his famous miracles and had private transport waiting for them, there wasn't any guarantee they'd make it back in time.

Still, Niko had to try. "Help me up and we can go."

Once Niko was on his feet and not wobbling too much, Rafe said, "That's not all."

"What?" Niko growled.

Rafe gave Niko a wary look. "Jaime Alvarez just got out of prison..."

DEAR READER

Thank you for reading *Undercover*. Did you enjoy learning how Niko's conflict with Alvarez got started? Their families have such a complicated history that I couldn't resist the opportunity to explore it in more detail.

Finally, if you enjoyed reading *Undercover*, please consider recommending it to family, friends, and anyone else you think might be interested in Niko's history with Alvarez.

Thank you for your support!

Happy reading!

Vanessa

UNDERCOVER
ACKNOWLEDGMENTS

A huge thank you to Kristin Miller, Jasmine Haynes, Valerie Susan Hayward and Angela Pike for helping make this a better book. Thanks also to Frauke Spanuth of Croco Designs for creating another awesome cover.

Most of all, my continuing gratitude to all the readers who have made this series a success!

ABOUT THE AUTHOR

Photo by Gigi Pandian

I confess. I spend way too much time thinking up ways to torture my characters. As a worst-case scenario thinker, I channel my persistently dark what-if questions into writing romantic thrillers that combine intense emotion with action-packed plots.

I'm best known for The Surgical Strike Unit series about a privately run special operations group. My new series, WAR, is set in West Africa, where I lived for a time.

When I'm not writing, listening to music, or playing puzzle games on my mobile device, I help writers learn Scrivener and take long hikes in the nearby hills.

JOIN THE KIERDEVILS

Receive snippets-of-life stories, writing updates, sneak peeks, and other exclusive content such as *The SSU/WAR Bonus Pack* when you join the KierDevils newsletter.

www.vanessakier.com/kierdevils